Boys Will Be Boys

Ruskin Bond has been writing for over sixty years, and now has over 120 titles in print—novels, collections of short stories, poetry, essays, anthologies and books for children. His first novel, *The Room on the Roof*, received the prestigious John Llewellyn Rhys Prize in 1957. He has also received the Padma Shri (1999), the Padma Bhushan (2014) and two awards from Sahitya Akademi—one for his short stories and another for his writings for children. In 2012, the Delhi government gave him its Lifetime Achievement Award.

Born in 1934, Ruskin Bond grew up in Jamnagar, Shimla, New Delhi and Dehradun. Apart from three years in the UK, he has spent all his life in India, and now lives in Mussoorie with his adopted family.

RUSKIN BOND

Boys Will Be Boys

RUPA

Published by
Rupa Publications India Pvt. Ltd 2021
7/16, Ansari Road, Daryaganj
New Delhi 110002

Sales centres:
Allahabad Bengaluru Chennai
Hyderabad Jaipur Kathmandu
Kolkata Mumbai

ISBN: 978-93-90918-98-0

First impression 2021

10 9 8 7 6 5 4 3 2 1

The moral right of the author has been asserted.

CONTENTS

INTRODUCTION

When adults face a particularly difficult situation in their lives, or when the routine of the everyday brings them down, they often reminisce about 'simpler times'. Times when the greatest worry was not having enough time on the playground, or having to face the wrath of a teacher because of a botched sum. Childhood memories can often bring solace to a burdened adult mind.

But as adults, we tend to forget how the problems that seem to us to be trivial, meant the end of the world to us as children. Your best friend not showing up for class, rain interrupting an intense hide and seek game or being the new kid in school, these were all problems that were very real, and very serious. Children are often seen as simple beings, and while innocent and without a malicious bone in their body, children too experience a range of emotions, and they experience them intensely.

This book tells the tale of friendship, of mischief and of finding your way in the world as a kid. It takes us through the things that intrigue young boys—trains, trees, animals and any opportunity to participate in mischief. It tells the tale of man-eating panthers, friendly leopards that hang out in tunnels, boys running from old women who are tired of them playing on their property, of surviving boarding school and finding family away from home. Set against the picturesque landscapes of the hills of North India, this book is for adults and children alike, for someone who needs to sit back and reminisce, and for someone who needs inspiration to make play time infinitely more fun!

Ruskin Bond

ROMI AND THE WILDFIRE

1

As Romi was about to mount his bicycle, he saw smoke rising from behind the distant line of trees.

'It looks like a forest fire,' said Prem, his friend and classmate.

'It's well to the east,' said Romi. 'Nowhere near the road.'

'There's a strong wind,' said Prem, looking at the dry leaves swirling across the road.

It was the middle of May, and it hadn't rained in the Terai for several weeks. The grass was brown, the leaves of the trees covered with dust. Even though it was getting on to six o'clock in the evening, the boys' shirts were damp with sweat.

'It will be getting dark soon,' said Prem. 'You'd better spend the night at my house.'

'No, I said I'd be home tonight. My father isn't keeping well. The doctor has given me some tablets for him.'

'You'd better hurry, then. That fire seems to be spreading.'

'Oh, it's far off. It will take me only forty minutes to ride through the forest. 'Bye, Prem—see you tomorrow!'

Romi mounted his bicycle and pedalled off down the main road of the village, scattering stray hens, stray dogs and stray villagers.

'Hey, look where you're going!' shouted an angry villager, leaping out of the way of the oncoming bicycle. 'Do you think you own the road?'

'Of course I own it,' called Romi cheerfully, and cycled on.

His own village lay about seven miles distant, on the other side of the forest; but there was only a primary school in his village, and Romi was now in High School. His father, who was a fairly wealthy sugarcane farmer, had only recently bought him the bicycle. Romi didn't care too much for school and felt there weren't enough holidays; but he enjoyed the long rides, and he got on well with his classmates.

He might have stayed the night with Prem had it not been for the tablets which the Vaid—the village doctor—had given him for his father.

Romi's father was having back trouble, and the medicine had been specially prepared from local herbs.

Having been given such a fine bicycle, Romi felt that the least he could do in return was to get those tablets to his father as early as possible.

He put his head down and rode swiftly out of the village. Ahead of him, the smoke rose from the burning forest and the sky glowed red.

2

He had soon left the village far behind. There was a slight climb, and Romi had to push harder on the pedals to get over the rise. Once over the top, the road went winding down to the edge of the sub-tropical forest.

This was the part Romi enjoyed most. He relaxed, stopped pedalling, and allowed the bicycle to glide gently down the slope. Soon the wind was rushing past him, blowing his hair about his face and making his shirt billow out behind. He burst into song.

A dog from the village ran beside him, barking furiously. Romi shouted at the dog, encouraging him in the race.

Then the road straightened out, and Romi began pedalling again.

The dog, seeing the forest ahead, turned back to the village. It was afraid of the forest.

The smoke was thicker now, and Romi caught the smell of burning timber. But ahead of him, the road was clear. He rode on.

It was a rough, dusty road, cut straight through the forest. Tall trees grew on either side, cutting off the last of the daylight. But the spreading glow of the fire on the right lit up the road, and giant tree-shadows danced before the boy on the bicycle.

Usually the road was deserted. This evening it was alive with wild creatures fleeing from the forest fire.

The first animal that Romi saw was a hare, leaping across the road in front of him. It was followed by several more hares. Then a band of monkeys streamed across, chattering excitedly.

They'll be safe on the other side, thought Romi. The fire won't cross the road.

But it was coming closer. And realising this, Romi pedalled harder. In half-an-hour he should be out of the forest.

Suddenly, from the side of the road, several pheasants rose in the air, and with a *whoosh*, flew low across the path, just in front of the oncoming bicycle. Taken by surprise, Romi fell off. When he picked himself up and began brushing his clothes, he saw that his knee was bleeding. It wasn't a deep cut, but he allowed it to bleed a little, took out his handkerchief and bandaged his knee. Then he mounted the bicycle again.

He rode a bit slower now, because birds and animals kept coming out of the bushes.

Not only pheasants but smaller birds, too, were streaming across the road—parrots, jungle crows, owls, magpies—and the air was filled with their cries.

'Everyone's on the move,' thought Romi. It must be a really big fire.

He could see the flames now, reaching out from behind the trees on his right, and he could hear the crackling as the dry leaves caught fire. The air was hot on his face. Leaves, still alight or turning to cinders, floated past.

A herd of deer crossed the road, and Romi had to stop until they had passed. Then he mounted again and rode on; but now, for the first time, he was feeling afraid.

3

From ahead came a faint clanging sound. It wasn't an animal sound, Romi was sure of that. A fire-engine? There were no fire-engines within fifty miles.

The clanging came nearer, and Romi discovered that the noise came from a small boy who was running along the forest path, two milk-cans clattering at his side

'Teju!' called Romi, recognising the boy from a neighbouring village. 'What are you doing out here?'

'Trying to get home, of course,' said Teju, panting along beside the bicycle.

'Jump on,' said Romi, stopping for him.

Teju was only eight or nine—a couple of years younger than Romi. He had come to deliver milk to some road-workers, but the workers had left at the first signs of the fire, and Teju was hurrying home with his cans still full of milk.

He got up on the cross-bar of the bicycle, and Romi moved on again. He was quite used to carrying friends on the crossbar.

'Keep beating your milk-cans,' said Romi. 'Like that, the animals will know we are coming. My bell doesn't make enough noise. I'm going to get a horn for my cycle!'

'I never knew there were so many animals in the jungle,' said Teju. 'I saw a python in the middle of the road. It stretched right across!'

'What did you do?'

'Just kept running and jumped right over it!'

Teju continued to chatter but Romi's thoughts were on the fire, which was much closer now. Flames shot up from the dry grass and ran up the trunks of trees and along the branches. Smoke billowed out above the forest.

Romi's eyes were smarting and his hair and eyebrows felt scorched. He was feeling tired but he couldn't stop now, he had to get beyond the range of the fire. Another ten or fifteen minutes of steady riding would get them to the small wooden bridge that spanned the little river separating the forest from the sugarcane fields.

Once across the river, they would be safe. The fire could not touch them on the other side, because the forest ended at the river's edge. But could they get to the river in time?

4

Clang, clang, clang, went Teju's milk-cans. But the sound of the fire grew louder too.

A tall silk-cotton tree, its branches leaning across the road, had caught fire. They were almost beneath it when there was a crash and a burning branch fell to the ground a few yards in front of them.

The boys had to get off the bicycle and leave the road, forcing their way through a tangle of thorny bushes on the left, dragging and pushing at the bicycle and only returning to the road some distance ahead of the burning tree.

'We won't get out in time,' said Teju, back on the cross-bar but feeling disheartened.

'Yes, we will,' said Romi, pedalling with all his might. 'The fire hasn't crossed the road as yet.'

Even as he spoke, he saw a small flame leap up from the grass on the left. It wouldn't be long before more sparks and burning leaves were blown across the road to kindle the grass on the other side.

'Oh, look!' exclaimed Romi, bringing the bicycle to a sudden stop.

'What's wrong now?' asked Teju, rubbing his sore eyes. And then, through the smoke, he saw what was stopping them.

An elephant was standing in the middle of the road.

Teju slipped off the cross-bar, his cans rolling on the ground, bursting open and spilling their contents.

The elephant was about forty feet away. It moved about restlessly, its big ears flapping as it turned its head from side to side, wondering which way to go.

From far to the left, where the forest was still untouched,

a herd of elephants moved towards the river. The leader of the herd raised his trunk and trumpeted a call. Hearing it, the elephant on the road raised its own trunk and trumpeted a reply. Then it shambled off into the forest, in the direction of the herd, leaving the way clear.

'Come, Teju, jump on!' urged Romi. 'We can't stay here much longer!'

5

Teju forgot about his milk-cans and pulled himself up on the cross-bar. Romi ran forward with the bicycle, to gain speed, and mounted swiftly. He kept as far as possible to the left of the road, trying to ignore the flames, the crackling, the smoke and the scorching heat.

It seemed that all the animals who could get away, had done so. The exodus across the road had stopped.

'We won't stop again,' said Romi, gritting his teeth. 'Not even for an elephant!'

'We're nearly there!' said Teju. He was perking up again.

A jackal, overcome by the heat and smoke, lay in the middle of the path, either dead or unconscious. Romi did not stop. He swerved round the animal. Then he put all his strength into one final effort.

He covered the last hundred yards at top speed, and then they were out of the forest, free-wheeling down the sloping road to the river.

'Look!' shouted Teju. 'The bridge is on fire!'

Burning embers had floated down on to the small wooden bridge, and the dry, ancient timber had quickly caught fire. It was now burning fiercely.

Romi did not hesitate. He left the road, riding the bicycle over sand and pebbles. Then with a rush they went down the river-bank and into the water.

The next thing they knew, they were splashing around, trying to find each other in the darkness.

'Help!' cried Teju. 'I'm drowning!'

6

'Don't be silly,' said Romi. 'The water isn't deep—it's only up to the knees. Come here and grab hold of me.'

Teju splashed across and grabbed Romi by the belt.

'The water's so cold,' he said, his teeth chattering.

'Do you want to go back and warm yourself?' asked Romi. 'Some people are never satisfied. Come on, help me get the bicycle up. It's down here, just where we are standing.'

Together they managed to heave the bicycle out of the water and stand it upright.

'Now sit on it,' said Romi. 'I'll push you across.'

'We'll be swept away,' said Teju.

'No, we won't. There's not much water in the river at this time of the year. But the current is quite strong in the middle, so sit still. All right?'

'All right,' said Teju nervously.

Romi began guiding the bicycle across the river, one hand on the seat and one hand on the handlebar. The river was shallow and sluggish in midsummer; even so, it was quite swift in the middle. But having got safely out of the burning forest, Romi was in no mood to let a little river defeat him.

He kicked off his shoes, knowing they would be lost; and then gripping the smooth stones of the river-bed with his toes, he concentrated on keeping his balance and getting the bicycle and Teju through the middle of the stream. The water here came up to his waist, and the current would have been too strong for Teju. But when they reached the shallows, Teju got down and helped Romi push the bicycle.

They reached the opposite bank, and sank down on the grass.

'We can rest now,' said Romi. 'But not all night—I've got some medicine to give to my father.' He felt in his pockets and found that the tablets in their envelope, had turned into a soggy mess. 'Oh well, he had to take them with water anyway,' he said.

They watched the fire as it continued to spread through the forest. It had crossed the road down which they had come. The sky was a bright red, and the river reflected the colour of the sky.

Several elephants had found their way down to the river. They were cooling off by spraying water on each other with their trunks. Further downstream there were deer and other animals.

Romi and Teju looked at each other in the glow from the fire. They hadn't known each other very well before. But now they felt they had been friends for years.

'What are you thinking about?' asked Teju.

'I'm thinking,' said Romi, 'that even if the fire is out in a day or two, it will be a long time before the bridge is repaired. So it will be a nice long holiday from school!'

'But you can walk across the river,' said Teju. 'You just did it.'

'Impossible,' said Romi. 'It's much too swift.'

FOUR BOYS ON A GLACIER

O n a day that promised rain we bundled ourselves into the bus that was to take us to Kapkote (where people lost their caps and coats, punned Anil), the starting-point of our Himalayan trek. I was seventeen at the time, and Anil and Somi were sixteen. Each of us carried a haversack, and we had also brought along a good-sized bedding-roll which, apart from blankets, contained bags of rice and flour, thoughtfully provided by Anil's mother. We had no idea how we would carry the bedding-roll once we started walking, but we didn't worry too much about details.

We were soon in the hills of Kumaon, on a winding road that took us up and up, until we saw the valley and our small town spread out beneath us, the river a silver ribbon across the plain. We took a sharp bend, the valley disappeared, and the mountains towered above us.

At Kapkote, we had refreshments and the shopkeeper told us we could spend the night in one of his rooms. The surroundings were pleasant, the hills wooded with deodars, the lower slopes planted with fresh green paddy. At night there was a wind moaning in the trees and it found its way through the cracks in the windows and eventually through our blankets.

Next morning we washed our faces at a small stream near

the shop and filled our water bottles for the day's march. A boy from the nearby village approached us, and asked where we were going.

'To the glacier,' said Somi.

'I'll come with you', said the boy. 'I know the way'

'You're too small,' said Anil. 'We need someone who can carry our bedding-roll.'

'I'm small but I'm strong,' said the boy, who certainly looked sturdy. He had pink cheeks and a well-knit body.

'See!' he said, and, picking up a rock the size of a football, he heaved it across the stream.

'I think he can come with us,' I said.

And then, we were walking—at first above the little Sarayu river, then climbing higher along the rough mule track, always within sound of the water, which we glimpsed now and then, swift, green and bubbling.

We were at the forest rest-house by six in the evening, after covering fifteen miles. Anil found the watchman asleep in a patch of fading sunlight and roused him. The watchman, who hadn't been bothered by visitors for weeks, grumbled at our intrusion but opened a room for us. He also produced some potatoes from his store, and these were roasted for dinner.

Just as we were about to get into our beds we heard a thud on the corrugated tin roof, and then the sound of someone—or something—scrambling about on the roof. Anil, Somi and I were alarmed; but Bisnu, who was already under the blankets, merely yawned, and turned over on his side.

'It's only a bear,' he said. 'Didn't you see the pumpkins on the roof? Bears love pumpkins.'

For half an hour we had to listen to the bear as it clambered about on the roof, feasting on the watchman's ripe pumpkins. At last there was silence. Anil and I crawled out of our blankets and went to the window. And through the frosted glass we saw a black Himalayan bear ambling across the slope in front of the house.

Our next rest-house lay in a narrow valley, on the banks of the rushing Pindar River, which twisted its way through the mountains. We walked on, past terraced fields and small stone houses, until there were no more fields or houses, only forest and sun and silence.

It was different from the silence of a room or an empty street.

And then, the silence broke into sound—the sound of the river.

Far down in the valley, the Pindar tumbled over itself in its impatience to reach the plains. We began to run; slipped and stumbled, but continued running.

The rest-house stood on a ledge just above the river, and the sound of the water rushing down the mountain-defile could be heard at all times. The sound of the birds, which we had grown used to, was drowned by the sound of the water, but the birds themselves could be seen, many-coloured, standing out splendidly against the dark green forest foliage—the red crowned jay, the paradise flycatcher, the purple whistling thrush and others we could not recognise.

Higher up the mountain, above some terraced land where oats and barley were grown, stood a small cluster of huts. This, we were told by the watchman, was the last village on the way to the glacier. It was, in fact, one of the last villages in India, because if we crossed the difficult passes beyond the glacier, we would find ourselves in Tibet.

Anil asked the watchman about the Abominable Snowman. The Nepalese believe in the existence of the Snowman, and our watchman was Nepalese.

'Yes, I have seen the yeti,' he told us. 'A great shaggy, flat-footed creature. In the winter, when it snows heavily, he passes the bungalow at night. I have seen his tracks the next morning.'

'Does he come this way in the summer?' asked Somi, anxiously.

'No,' said the watchman. 'But sometimes I have seen the *lidini*. You have to be careful of her.'

'And who is the *lidini*?' asked Anil.

'She is the snow-woman, and far more dangerous. She has the same height as the yeti—about seven feet when her back is straight—and her hair is much longer. Also she has very long teeth. Her feet face inwards, but she can run very fast, especially downhill. If you see a lidini, and she chases you, always run in an uphill direction. She tires quickly because of her crooked feet. But when running downhill she has no trouble at all, and you want to be very fast to escape her!'

'Well, we are quite fast,' said Anil with a nervous laugh. 'But its just a fairy-story, I don't believe a word of it.'

The watchman was most offended, and refused to tell us anything more about snowmen and snow-women. But he helped Bisnu make a fire, and presented us with a black, sticky sweet, which we ate with relish.

It was a fine, sunny morning when we set out to cover the last seven miles to the glacier. We had expected a stiff climb, but the rest-house was 11,000 feet above sea-level, and the rest of the climb was fairly gradual.

Suddenly, abruptly, there were no more trees. As the bungalow dropped out of sight, the trees and bushes gave way to short grass and little pink and blue alpine flowers. The snow peaks were close now, ringing us in on every side. We passed white waterfalls, cascading hundreds of feet down precipitous rock faces, thundering into the little river. A great white eagle hovered over us.

The hill fell away, and there, confronting us, was a great white field of snow and ice, cradled between two shining peaks. We were speechless for several minutes. Then we proceeded cautiously on to the snow, supporting each other on the slippery surface. We could not go far, because we were quite unequipped for any high-altitude climbing. But it was a satisfying feeling to know that we were the only young men from our town who had walked so far and so high.

The sun was reflected sharply from the snow and we felt surprisingly warm. It was delicious to feel the sun crawling over our bodies, sinking deep into our bones. Meanwhile, almost imperceptibly, clouds had covered some of the peaks, and white mist drifted down the mountain slopes. It was time to return: we would barely make it to the bungalow before it grew dark.

We took our time returning to Kapkote; stopped by the Sarayu River; bathed with the village boys we had seen on the way up; collected strawberries and ferns and wild flowers; and finally said goodbye to Bisnu.

Anil wanted to take Bisnu along with us, but the boy's parents refused to let him go, saying that he was too young for the life of a city.

'Never mind,' said Somi. 'We'll go on another trek next year, and we'll take you with us, Bisnu.'

This promise pleased Bisnu, and he saw us off at the bus-stop, shouldering our bedding-roll to the end. Then he climbed a pine tree to have a better view of us leaving. We saw him waving to us from the tree as the bus went round the bend from Kapkote, and then the hills were left behind and the plains stretched out below.

RANJI'S WONDERFUL BAT

'How's that!' shouted the wicket-keeper, holding the ball up in his gloves.

'How's that!' echoed the slip fielders.

'How?' growled the fast bowler, glaring at the umpire.

'Out!' said the umpire.

And Suraj, the captain of the school team, walked slowly back to the pavilion—which was really a tool-shed at the end of the field.

The score stood at 53 for 4 wickets. Another sixty runs had to be made for victory, and only one good batsman remained. All the rest were bowlers who couldn't be expected to make many runs.

It was Ranji's turn to bat.

He was the youngest member of the team, only eleven, but sturdy and full of pluck. As he walked briskly to the wicket, his unruly black hair was blown about by a cool breeze that came down from the hills.

Ranji had a good eye and strong wrists, and had made lots of runs in some of the minor matches. But in the last two inter-school games his scores had been poor, the highest being twelve runs. Now he was determined to make enough runs to take his side to victory.

Ranji took his guard and prepared to face the bowler. The fielders moved closer, in anticipation of another catch. The tall fast bowler scowled and began his long run. His arm whirled and the hard shiny red ball came hurling towards Ranji.

Ranji was going to lunge forward and play the ball back to the bowler, but at the last moment he changed his mind and stepped back, intending to push the ball through the ring of fielders on his right or off-side. The ball swung in the air, shot off the grass and came through sharply to strike Ranji on his pads.

'How's that!' screamed the bowler, hopping about like a kangaroo.

'How!' shouted the wicket-keeper. 'How?' asked all the fielders. The umpire slowly raised a finger.

'Out,' he said.

And it was Ranji's turn to walk back to the tool-shed.

The match was won by the visiting team.

'Never mind,' said Suraj, patting Ranji on the back. 'You'll do better next time. You're out of form just now, that's all.'

But their cricket coach was sterner.

'You'll have to make more runs in the next game,' he warned Ranji, 'or you'll lose your place in the side!'

Avoiding the other players, Ranji walked slowly homewards, his head down, his hands in his pockets. He was very upset. He had been trying so hard and practising regularly, but when an important game came along he failed to make a big score. It seemed that there was nothing he could do about it. But he loved playing cricket, and he couldn't bear the thought of being out of the school team.

On his way home he had to pass the clock tower. He often stopped at Mr Kumar's Sports Shop, to chat with the owner or look at all the things on the shelves: footballs, cricket balls, badminton rackets, hockey sticks, balls of various shapes and sizes. It was a wonderland where Ranji usually liked to linger. But this was one day when he didn't feel like stopping. He looked the other way and was about to cross the road when Mr Kumar's voice stopped him.

'Hello, Ranji! Off in a hurry today? And why are you looking so sad?'

So, Ranji had to stop and say namaste. He couldn't ignore Mr Kumar, who had been so kind and helpful, always giving him advice on how to play different kinds of bowling. Mr Kumar had been a state player once, and had scored a century in a match against Tanzania. Now he was too old for first-class cricket, but he liked encouraging young players and he thought Ranji would make a good cricketer.

'What's the trouble?' he asked, as Ranji stepped into the shop. 'Lost the game today?'

Ranji felt better as soon as he was inside the shop. Mr Kumar was so friendly, even the sports goods seemed friendly. The bats and balls and shuttle-cocks all seemed to want to be helpful.

'We lost the match,' said Ranji.

'Never mind,' said Mr Kumar. 'Where would we be without losers? There wouldn't be any games without them—no cricket or football or hockey or tennis! No carom or marbles. No sports shop for me! Anyway, how many runs did you make?'

'None. I made a big round egg.'

Mr Kumar rested his hand on Ranji's shoulder. 'Never mind. All good players have a bad day now and then.'

'But I haven't made a good score in my last three matches,' said Ranji. 'I'll be dropped from the team if I don't do something in the next game.'

'Well, we can't let that happen,' mused Mr Kumar. 'Something will have to be done about it.'

'I'm just unlucky,' said Ranji.

'Maybe, maybe...But in that case, it's time your luck changed.'

'It's too late now,' said Ranji.

'Nonsense. It's never too late. Now you just come with me to the back of my shop and I'll see if I can do something about your luck.'

Puzzled, Ranji followed Mr Kumar through the curtained partition at the back of the shop. He found himself in a badly-lit room stacked to the ceiling with all kinds of old and second-hand sporting goods—torn football bladders, broken bats, rackets without strings, broken darts and tattered badminton nets.

Mr Kumar began examining a number of old cricket bats, and after a few minutes he said 'Ah!' and picked up one of the bats. Held it out to Ranji. 'This is it,' he said.

'This is the luckiest of all my old bats. This is the bat I made a century with!'

And he gave it a twirl and started hitting an imaginary ball to all corners of the room.

'Of course, it's an old bat, but it hasn't lost any of its magic,' said Mr Kumar, pausing in his stroke-making to recover his breath. He held it out to Ranji again. 'Here, take it! I'll lend it to you for the rest of the cricket season. You won't fail with it.'

Ranji took the bat and gazed at it with awe and delight.

'Is it really the bat you made a century with?' he asked.

'It is,' said Mr Kumar. 'And it may get you a hundred runs too!'

Ranji spent a nervous week waiting for Saturday's match. His school team would be playing a strong side from another town. There was a lot of class work that week, so Ranji did not get much time to practice with the other boys. As he had no brothers or sisters, he asked Koki, the girl next door, to bowl to him in the garden. Koki bowled quite well, but Ranji liked to hit the ball hard—'just to get used to the bat,' he told her—and she soon got tired of chasing the ball all over the garden.

At last Saturday arrived, bright and sunny and just right for cricket.

Suraj won the toss for the school and decided to bat first.

The opening batsmen scored thirty runs without being separated. The visiting fast bowlers couldn't do much. The spin bowlers came on, and immediately there was a change in the game. Two wickets fell in one over, and the score was 33 for 2. Suraj made a few quick runs, then he too got out to one of the spinners, caught behind the wicket. The next batsman was clean bowled—46 for 4—and it was Ranji's turn to bat.

He walked slowly to the wicket. The fielders crowded round him. He took guard and prepared for the first ball.

The bowler took a short run and then the ball was twirling towards Ranji, looking as though it would spin away from his bat as he leant forward into his stroke.

And then a thrill ran through Ranji's arm as he felt the ball meet the springy willow of the bat.

Crack!

The ball, hit firmly with the middle of Ranji's bat, streaked past the helpless bowler and sped towards the boundary. Four runs!

The bowler was annoyed, with the result that his next ball was a loose full toss. Ranji swung it to the on-side boundary for another four.

And that was only the beginning. Now Ranji began to play

all the strokes he knew: late cuts, square cuts, straight drives, on-drives and off-drives. The rival captain tried all his bowlers, fast and spin, but none of them could remove Ranji, who sent the fielders scampering all over the field.

At the lunch break he had scored forty. And twenty minutes after lunch, when Suraj closed the innings, Ranji was not out with fifty-eight.

The rival team was bowled out for a poor score, and Ranji's school won the match.

On his way home, Ranji stopped at Mr Kumar's shop to give him. the good news.

'We won!' he said. And I made fifty-eight—my highest score so far. It really is a lucky bat!'

'I told you so,' said Mr Kumar, giving Ranji a warm handshake. 'There'll be bigger scores yet.'

Ranji went home in high spirits. He was so pleased that he stopped at the Jumna Sweet Shop and bought two laddoos for Koki. She liked cricket but she liked laddoos even more.

Mr Kumar was right. Ranji's performance that day was only the beginning of Ranji's success with the bat. In the next game he scored forty but then, he grew careless and allowed himself to be stumped by the wicket-keeper. The game that followed was a two-day match, and Ranji, who was now batting at number 3, made forty-five runs. He hit several boundaries before being caught. In the second innings, when the school team needed only sixty runs for victory, Ranji was batting on twenty-five when the winning runs were hit.

Everyone was pleased with him—his coach, his captain Suraj and Mr Kumar—but the lucky bat remained a secret between Ranji and Mr Kumar.

One evening, during an informal game on the maidan,

Ranji's friend Bhim slipped while running after the ball, and cut his hand on a sharp stone. Ranji took him to a doctor near the clock tower, where the wound was washed and bandaged. As it was getting late, he decided to go straight home. Usually he walked, but that evening Ranji caught a bus near the clock tower.

When he got home, his mother brought him a cup of tea and while he was drinking it, Koki walked in. The first thing she said was, 'Ranji, where's your bat?'

'Oh, I must have left it on the maidan when Bhim got hurt,' said Ranji, starting up and spilling his tea. 'I'd better go and get it now, or it will disappear.'

'You can fetch it tomorrow,' said his mother. 'It's getting dark.'

'I'll take a torch,' said Ranji.

He was worried about the bat. Without it, his luck might desert him. He hadn't the patience to wait for a bus, and ran all the way to the maidan.

The maidan was deserted and there was no sign of the bat. Then Ranji remembered that he'd had it with him on the bus, after saying goodbye to Bhim at the clock tower. He must have left it on the bus!

Well, he'd never find it now. The bat was lost forever. And on Saturday Ranji's school would be playing their last and most important match of the cricket season, against a visiting team from Delhi.

Next day, he was at Mr Kumar's shop, looking very sorry for himself.

'What's the matter?' asked Mr Kumar.

'I've lost the bat,' said Ranji. 'Your lucky bat. The one I made all those runs with! I left it on the bus. And the day after tomorrow we are playing the Delhi school, and I'll be out for a duck, and we'll lose our chance of being the school champions.'

Mr Kumar looked a little anxious at first; then he smiled and said, 'You can still make all the runs you want.'

'But I don't have the bat any more,' said Ranji.

'Any bat will do,' said Mr Kumar.

'What do you mean?'

'I mean it's the batsman and not the bat that matters. Shall I tell you something? That old bat I gave you was no different from any other bat I've used. True, I made lots of runs with it, but I made runs with other bats too. I never depended on a special bat for my runs. A bat has magic only when the batsman has magic! What you needed was confidence, not a bat. And by believing in the bat, you got your confidence back!'

'What's confidence?' asked Ranji. It was a new word for him.

'Con-fi-dence,' said Mr Kumar slowly. 'Confidence is knowing you are good.'

'And I can be good without the bat?'

'Of course. You have always been good. You are good now. You will be good the day after tomorrow. Remember that. If you do, you'll make the runs.'

On Saturday Ranji walked to the wicket with a bat borrowed from Bhim.

The school team had lost its first wicket with only two runs on the board. Ranji went in at this stage. The Delhi school's opening bowler was sending down some really fast ones. Ranji faced him confidently.

The first ball was very fast but it wasn't a good length. Quick on his feet, Ranji stepped back and pulled it hard to the on-boundary. The ball soared over the heads of the fielders and landed with a crash in a crate of cold drink bottles.

A six! Everyone stood up and cheered.

It was the start of Ranji's wonderful innings. The match ended in a draw, but Ranji's seventy-five was the talk of the school.

On his way home he bought a dozen laddoos, ten for Koki—and ten for Mr Kumar.

THE FIGHT

Ranji had been less than a month in Rajpur when he discovered the pool in the forest. It was the height of summer, and his school had not yet opened, and, having as yet made no friends in this semi-hill station, he wandered about a good deal by himself into the hills and forests that stretched away interminably on all sides of the town. It was hot, very hot, at that time of year, and Ranji walked about in his vest and shorts, his brown feet white with the chalky dust that flew up from the ground. The earth was parched, the grass brown, the trees listless, hardly stirring, waiting for a cool wind or a refreshing shower of rain.

It was on such a day—a hot, tired day—that Ranji found the pool in the forest. The water had a gentle translucency, and you could see the smooth round pebbles at the bottom of the pool. A small stream emerged from a cluster of rocks to feed the pool. During the monsoon, this stream would be a gushing torrent, cascading down from the hills, but during the summer it was barely a trickle. The rocks, however, held the water in the pool, and it did not dry up like the pools in the plains.

When Ranji saw the pool, he did not hesitate to get into it. He had often gone swimming, alone or with friends, when he had lived with his parents in a thirsty town in the middle of the Rajputana desert. There, he had known only sticky, muddy pools, where buffaloes wallowed and women washed clothes. He had never seen a pool like this—so clean and cold and inviting. He threw off all his clothes, as he had done when he went swimming in the plains, and leapt into the water. His limbs were supple, free of any fat, and his dark body glistened in patches of sunlit water.

The next day he came again to quench his body in the cool waters of the forest pool. He was there for almost an hour, sliding in and out of the limpid green water, or lying stretched out on the smooth yellow rocks in the shade of broad-leaved sal trees. It was while he lay thus, naked on a rock, that he noticed another boy standing a little distance away, staring at him in a rather hostile manner. The other boy was a little older than Ranji, taller, thick-set, with a broad nose and thick, red lips. He had only just noticed Ranji, and he stood at the edge of the pool, wearing a pair of bathing shorts, waiting for Ranji to explain himself.

When Ranji did not say anything, the other called out, 'What are you doing here, Mister?'

Ranji, who was prepared to be friendly, was taken aback at the hostility of the other's tone.

'I am swimming,' he replied. 'Why don't you join me?'

'I always swim alone,' said the other. 'This is my pool, I did not invite you here. And why are you not wearing any clothes?'

'It is not your business if I do not wear clothes. I have nothing to be ashamed of.'

'You skinny fellow, put on your clothes.'

'Fat fool, take yours off.'

This was too much for the stranger to tolerate. He strode

up to Ranji, who still sat on the rock and, planting his broad feet firmly on the sand, said (as though this would settle the matter once and for all), 'Don't you know I am a Punjabi? I do not take replies from villagers like you!'

'So you like to fight with villagers?' said Ranji. 'Well, I am not a villager. I am a Rajput!'

'I am a Punjabi!'

'I am a Rajput!'

They had reached an impasse. One had said he was a Punjabi, the other had proclaimed himself a Rajput. There was little else that could be said.

'You understand that I am a Punjabi?' said the stranger, feeling that perhaps this information had not penetrated Ranji's head.

'I have heard you say it three times,' replied Ranji.

'Then why are you not running away?'

'I am waiting for *you* to run away!'

'I will have to beat you,' said the stranger, assuming a violent attitude, showing Ranji the palm of his hand.

'I am waiting to see you do it,' said Ranji.

'You will see me do it,' said the other boy.

Ranji waited. The other boy made a strange, hissing sound. They stared each other in the eye for almost a minute. Then the Punjabi boy slapped Ranji across the face with all the force he could muster. Ranji staggered, feeling quite dizzy. There were thick red finger marks on his cheek.

'There you are!' exclaimed his assailant. 'Will you be off now?'

For answer, Ranji swung his arm up and pushed a hard, bony fist into the other's face.

And then they were at each other's throats, swaying on

the rock, tumbling on to the sand, rolling over and over, their legs and arms locked in a desperate, violent struggle. Gasping and cursing, clawing and slapping, they rolled right into the shallows of the pool.

Even in the water the fight continued as, spluttering and covered with mud, they groped for each other's head and throat. But after five minutes of frenzied, unscientific struggle, neither boy had emerged victorious. Their bodies heaving with exhaustion, they stood back from each other, making tremendous efforts to speak.

'Now...now do you realise...I am a Punjabi?' gasped the stranger.

'Do you know I am a Rajput?' said Ranji with difficulty.

They gave a moment's consideration to each other's answers, and in that moment of silence there was only their heavy breathing and the rapid beating of their hearts.

'Then you will not leave the pool?' said the Punjabi boy.

'I will not leave it,' said Ranji.

'Then we shall have to continue the fight,' said the other.

'All right,' said Ranji.

But neither boy moved, neither took the initiative.

The Punjabi boy had an inspiration.

'We will continue the fight tomorrow,' he said. 'If you dare to come here again tomorrow, we will continue this fight, and I will not show you mercy as I have done today.'

'I will come tomorrow,' said Ranji. 'I will be ready for you.'

They turned from each other then and, going to their respective rocks, put on their clothes, and left the forest by different routes.

When Ranji got home, he found it difficult to explain the cuts and bruises that showed on his face, legs and arms. It was difficult to conceal the fact that he had been in an unusually violent fight, and his mother insisted on his staying at home for the rest of the day. That evening, though, he slipped out of the house and went to the bazaar, where he found comfort and solace in a bottle of vividly coloured lemonade and a banana leaf full of hot, sweet jalebis. He had just finished the lemonade when he saw his adversary coming down the road. His first impulse was to turn away and look elsewhere, his second to throw the lemonade bottle at his enemy. But he did neither of these things. Instead, he stood his ground and scowled at his passing adversary. And the Punjabi boy said nothing either, but scowled back with equal ferocity.

The next day was as hot as the previous one. Ranji felt weak and lazy and not at all eager for a fight. His body was stiff and sore after the previous day's encounter. But he could not refuse the challenge. Not to turn up at the pool would be an acknowledgement of defeat. From the way he felt just then, he knew he would be beaten in another fight. But he could not acquiesce in his own defeat. He must defy his enemy to the last, or outwit him, for only then could he gain his respect. If he surrendered now, he would be beaten for all time; but to fight and be beaten today left him free to fight and be beaten again. As long as he fought, he had a right to the pool in the forest.

He was half hoping that the Punjabi boy would have forgotten the challenge, but these hopes were dashed when he saw his opponent sitting, stripped to the waist, on a rock on the other side of the pool. The Punjabi boy was rubbing oil on his body, massaging it into his broad thighs. He saw Ranji beneath the sal trees, and called a challenge across the waters of the pool.

'Come over on this side and fight!' he shouted.

But Ranji was not going to submit to any conditions laid down by his opponent.

'Come *this* side and fight!' he shouted back with equal vigour.

'Swim across and fight me here!' called the other. 'Or perhaps you cannot swim the length of this pool?'

But Ranji could have swum the length of the pool a dozen times without tiring, and here he would show the Punjabi boy his superiority. So, slipping out of his vest and shorts, he dived straight into the water, cutting through it like a knife, and surfaced with hardly a splash. The Punjabi boy's mouth hung open in amazement.

'You can dive!' he exclaimed.

'It is easy,' said Ranji, treading water, waiting for a further challenge. 'Can't you dive?'

'No,' said the other. 'I jump straight in. But if you will tell me how, I will make a dive.'

'It is easy,' said Ranji. 'Stand on the rock, stretch your arms out and allow your head to displace your feet.'

The Punjabi boy stood up, stiff and straight, stretched out his arms, and threw himself into the water. He landed flat on his belly, with a crash that sent the birds screaming out of the trees.

Ranji dissolved into laughter.

'Are you trying to empty the pool?' he asked, as the Punjabi boy came to the surface, spouting water like a small whale.

'Wasn't it good?' asked the boy, evidently proud of his feat.

'Not very good,' said Ranji. 'You should have more practice. See, I will do it again.'

And pulling himself up on a rock, he executed another perfect dive. The other boy waited for him to come up, but,

swimming under water, Ranji circled him and came upon him
from behind.

'How did you do that?' asked the astonished youth.

'Can't you swim under water?' asked Ranji.

'No, but I will try it.'

The Punjabi boy made a tremendous effort to plunge to
the bottom of the pool and indeed he thought he had gone
right down, though his bottom, like a duck's, remained above
the surface.

Ranji, however, did not discourage him.

'It was not bad,' he said. 'But you need a lot of practice.'

'Will you teach me?' asked his enemy.

'If you like, I will teach you.'

'You must teach me. If you do not teach me, I will beat
you. Will you come here every day and teach me?'

'If you like,' said Ranji. They had pulled themselves out of
the water, and were sitting side by side on a smooth grey rock.

'My name is Suraj,' said the Punjabi boy. 'What is yours?'

'It is Ranji.'

'I am strong, am I not?' asked Suraj, bending his arm so
that a ball of muscle stood up stretching the white of his flesh.

'You are strong,' said Ranji. 'You are a real pahelwan.'

'One day I will be the world's champion wrestler,' said
Suraj, slapping his thighs, which shook with the impact of his
hand. He looked critically at Ranji's hard thin body. 'You are
quite strong yourself,' he conceded. 'But you are too bony. I
know, you people do not eat enough. You must come and have
your food with me.

I drink one *seer* of milk every day. We have got our own
cow! Be my friend, and I will make you a pahelwan like me!
I know—if you teach me to dive and swim underwater, I will

make you a pahelwan! That is fair, isn't it?'

'That is fair!' said Ranji, though he doubted if he was getting the better of the exchange.

Suraj put his arm around the younger boy and said, 'We are friends now, yes?'

They looked at each other with honest, unflinching eyes, and in that moment love and understanding were born.

'We are friends,' said Ranji.

The birds had settled again on their branches, and the pool was quiet and limpid in the shade of the sal trees.

'It is our pool,' said Suraj. 'Nobody else can come here without our permission. Who would dare?'

'Who would dare?' said Ranji, smiling with the knowledge that he had won the day.

THE TUNNEL

It was almost noon, and the jungle was very still, very silent. Heat waves shimmered along the railway embankment where it cut a path through the tall evergreen trees. The railway lines were two straight black serpents disappearing into the tunnel in the hillside.

Suraj stood near the cutting, waiting for the mid-day train. It wasn't a station, and he wasn't catching a train. He was waiting so that he could watch the steam-engine come roaring out of the tunnel.

He had cycled out of the town and taken the jungle path until he had come to a small village. He had left the cycle there, and walked over a low, scrub-covered hill and down to the tunnel exit.

Now he looked up. He had heard, in the distance, the shrill whistle of the engine. He couldn't see anything, because the train was approaching from the other side of the hill; but presently a sound, like distant thunder, issued from the tunnel, and he knew the train was coming through.

A second or two later, the steam-engine shot out of the tunnel, snorting and puffing like some green, black and gold dragon, some beautiful monster out of Suraj's dreams.

Showering sparks left and right, it roared a challenge to the jungle.

Instinctively, Suraj stepped back a few paces. And then the train had gone, leaving only a plume of smoke to drift lazily over tall shisham trees.

The jungle was still again. No one moved. Suraj turned from his contemplation of the drifting smoke and began walking along the embankment towards the tunnel.

The tunnel grew darker as he walked further into it. When he had gone about twenty yards, it became pitch black. Suraj had to turn and look back at the opening to reassure himself that there was still daylight outside. Ahead of him, the tunnel's other opening was just a small round circle of light.

The tunnel was still full of smoke from the train, but it would be several hours before another train came through. Till then, it belonged to the jungle again.

Suraj didn't stop, because there was nothing to do in the tunnel and nothing to see. He had simply wanted to walk through, so that he would know what the inside of a tunnel was really like. The walls were damp and sticky. A bat flew past. A lizard scuttled between the lines.

Coming straight from the darkness into the light, Suraj was dazzled by the sudden glare. He put a hand up to shade his eyes and looked up at the tree-covered hillside. He thought he saw something moving between the trees.

It was just a flash of orange and gold, and a long swishing tail. It was there between the trees for a second or two, and then it was gone.

About fifty feet from the entrance to the tunnel stood the watchman's hut. Marigolds grew in front of the hut, and at the back there was a small vegetable patch. It was the watchman's duty to inspect the tunnel and keep it clear of obstacles. Every day, before the train came through, he would walk the length of the tunnel. If all was well, he would return to his hut and take a nap. If something was wrong, he would walk back up the line and wave a red flag and the engine-driver would slow down. At night, the watchman lit an oil lamp and made a similar inspection of the tunnel. Of course, he could not stop the train if there was a porcupine on the line. But if there was any danger to the train, he'd go back up the line and wave his lamp to the approaching engine. If all was well, he'd hang his lamp at the door of the hut and go to sleep.

He was just settling down on his cot for an afternoon nap when he saw the boy emerge from the tunnel. He waited until Suraj was only a few feet away and then said: 'Welcome, welcome, I don't often have visitors. Sit down for a while, and tell me why you were inspecting my tunnel.'

'Is it your tunnel?' asked Suraj.

'It is,' said the watchman. 'It is truly my tunnel, since no one else will have anything to do with it. I have only lent it to the government.'

Suraj sat down on the edge of the cot.

'I wanted to see the train come through,' he said. 'And then, when it had gone, I thought I'd walk through the tunnel.'

'And what did you find in it?'

'Nothing. It was very dark. But when I came out, I thought I saw an animal—up on the hill—but I'm not sure, it moved away very quickly.'

'It was a leopard you saw,' said the watchman. 'My leopard.'

'Do you own a leopard too?'

'I do.'

'And do you lend it to the government?'

'I do not.'

'Is it dangerous?'

'No, it's a leopard that minds its own business. It comes to this range for a few days every month.'

'Have you been here a long time?' asked Suraj.

'Many years. My name is Sunder Singh.'

'My name's Suraj.'

'There's one train during the day. And another during the night. Have you seen the night mail come through the tunnel?'

'No. At what time does it come?'

'About nine o'clock, if it isn't late. You could come and sit here with me, if you like. And after it has gone, I'll take you home.'

'I shall ask my parents,' said Suraj. 'Will it be safe?'

'Of course. It's safer in the jungle than in the town. Nothing happens to me out here, but last month when I went into the town, I was almost run over by a bus.'

Sunder Singh yawned and stretched himself out on the cot. 'And now I'm going to take a nap, my friend. It is too hot to be up and about in the afternoon.'

'Everyone goes to sleep in the afternoon,' complained Suraj. 'My father lies down as soon as he's had his lunch.'

'Well, the animals also rest in the heat of the day. It is only the tribe of boys who cannot, or will not, rest.'

Sunder Singh placed a large banana-leaf over his face to keep away the flies, and was soon snoring gently. Suraj stood up, looking up and down the railway tracks. Then he began walking back to the village.

The following evening, towards dusk, as the flying foxes swooped silently out of the trees, Suraj made his way to the watchman's hut.

It had been a long hot day, but now the earth was cooling, and a light breeze was moving through the trees. It carried with it a scent of mango blossoms, the promise of rain.

Sunder Singh was waiting for Suraj. He had watered his small garden, and the flowers looked cool and fresh. A kettle was boiling on a small oil-stove.

'I'm making tea,' he said. 'There's nothing like a glass of hot tea while waiting for a train.'

They drank their tea, listening to the sharp notes of the tailorbird and the noisy chatter of the seven-sisters. As the brief twilight faded, most of the birds fell silent. Sunder Singh lit his oil-lamp and said it was time for him to inspect the tunnel. He moved off towards the tunnel, while Suraj sat on the cot, sipping his tea. In the dark, the trees seemed to move closer to him. And the night life of the forest was conveyed on the breeze—the sharp call of a barking-deer, the cry of a fox, the quaint tonk-tonk of a nightjar. There were some sounds that Suraj couldn't recognise—sounds that came from the trees, creakings and whisperings, as though the trees were coming alive, stretching their limbs in the dark, shifting a little, reflexing their fingers.

Sunder Singh stood inside the tunnel, trimming his lamp. The night sounds were familiar to him and he did not give them much thought; but something else—a padded footfall, a rustle of dry leaves—made him stand alert for a few seconds, peering into the darkness. Then, humming softly to himself, he returned to where Suraj was waiting. Another ten minutes remained for the night mail to arrive.

As Sunder Singh sat down on the cot beside Suraj, a new sound reached both of them quite distinctly—a rhythmic sawing sound, as if someone was cutting through the branch of a tree.

'What's that?' whispered Suraj.

'It's the leopard,' said Sunder Singh.

'I think it's in the tunnel.'

'The train will soon be here,' reminded Suraj.

'Yes, my friend. And if we don't drive the leopard out of the tunnel, it will be run over and killed. I can't let that happen.'

'But won't it attack us if we try to drive it out?' asked Suraj, beginning to share the watchman's concern.

'Not this leopard. It knows me well. We have seen each other many times. It has a weakness for goats and stray dogs, but it won't harm us. Even so, I'll take my axe with me. You stay here, Suraj.'

'No, I'm going with you. It'll be better than sitting here alone in the dark!'

'All right, but stay close behind me. And remember, there's nothing to fear.'

Raising his lamp high, Sunder Singh advanced into the tunnel, shouting at the top of his voice to try and scare away the animal. Suraj followed close behind, but he found he was unable to do any shouting. His throat was quite dry.

They had gone just about twenty paces into the tunnel when the light from the lamp fell upon the leopard. It was crouching between the tracks, only fifteen feet away from them. It was not a very big leopard, but it looked lithe and sinewy. Baring its teeth and snarling, it went down on its belly, tail twitching.

Suraj and Sunder Singh both shouted together. Their voices rang through the tunnel. And the leopard, uncertain as to how many terrifying humans were there in the tunnel with him, turned swiftly and disappeared into the darkness.

To make sure that it had gone, Sunder Singh and Suraj walked the length of the tunnel. When they returned to the entrance, the rails were beginning to hum. They knew the train was coming.

Suraj put his hand to the rails and felt its tremor. He heard the distant rumble of the train. And then the engine came round the bend, hissing at them, scattering sparks into the darkness, defying the jungle as it roared through the steep sides of the cutting. It charged straight at the tunnel, and into it, thundering past Suraj like the beautiful dragon of his dreams.

And when it had gone, the silence returned and the forest seemed to breathe, to live again. Only the rails still trembled with the passing of the train.

And they trembled to the passing of the same train, almost a week later, when Suraj and his father were both travelling in it.

Suraj's father was scribbling in a notebook, doing his accounts. Suraj sat at an open window staring out at the darkness. His father was going to Delhi on a business trip and had decided to take the boy along. 'I don't know where he gets to, most of the time,' he'd complained. 'I think it's time he learnt something about my business.'

The night mail rushed through the forest with its hundreds of passengers. Tiny flickering lights came and went, as they passed small villages on the fringe of the jungle.

Suraj heard the rumble as the train passed over a small bridge. It was too dark to see the hut near the cutting, but he knew they must be approaching the tunnel. He strained his eyes looking out into the night; and then, just as the engine let out a shrill whistle, Suraj saw the lamp.

He couldn't see Sunder Singh, but he saw the lamp, and he knew that his friend was out there.

The train went into the tunnel and out again; it left the jungle behind and thundered across the endless plains; and Suraj stared out at the darkness, thinking of the lonely cutting in the forest, and the watchman with the lamp who would always remain a firefly for those travelling thousands, as he lit up the darkness for steam-engines and leopards.

THE GREAT TRAIN JOURNEY

Suraj waved to a passing train, and kept waving until only the spiralling smoke remained. He liked waving to trains. He wondered about the people in them, and about where they were going and what it would be like there. And when the train had passed, leaving behind only the hot, empty track, Suraj was lonely.

He was a little lonely now. His hands in his pockets, he wandered along the railway track, kicking at loose pebbles and sending them down the bank. Soon there were other tracks, a railway-siding, a stationary goods train.

Suraj walked the length of the goods train. The carriage doors were closed and, as there were no windows, he couldn't see inside. He looked around to see if he was observed, and then, satisfied that he was alone, began trying the doors. He was almost at the end of the train when a carriage door gave way to his thrust.

It was dark inside the carriage. Suraj stood outside in the bright sunlight, peering into the darkness, trying to recognise bulky, shapeless objects. He stepped into the carriage and felt around. The objects were crates, and through the cross-section of woodwork he felt straw. He opened the other door and the

sun streamed into the compartment, driving out the musty
darkness.

Suraj sat down on a packing-case, his chin cupped in his
hands. The school was closed for the summer holidays, and he
had been wandering about all day and still did not know what to
do with himself. The carriage was bare of any sort of glamour.
Passing trains fascinated him—moving trains, crowded trains,
shrieking, panting trains all fascinated him—but this smelly, dark
compartment filled him only with gloom and more loneliness.

He did not really look gloomy or lonely. He looked fierce
at times, when he glared out at people from under his dark
eyebrows, but otherwise he usually wore a contented look—and
no one could guess just how deep his thoughts were!

Perhaps, if he had company, some fun could be had in
the carriage. If there had been a friend with him, someone
like Ranji...

He looked at the crates. He was always curious about things
that were bolted or nailed down or in some way concealed
from him—things like parcels and locked rooms—and carriage
doors and crates!

He went from one crate to another, and soon his perseverance
was rewarded. The cover of one hadn't been properly nailed
down. Suraj got his fingers under the edge and prised up the
lid. Absorbed in this operation, he did not notice the slight
shudder that passed through the train.

He plunged his hands into the straw and pulled out an apple.

It was a dark, ruby-red apple, and it lay in the dusty palm
of Suraj's hand like some gigantic precious stone, smooth and
round and glowing in the sunlight. Suraj looked up, out of the
doorway, and thought he saw a tree walking past the train.

He dropped the apple and stared.

There was another tree, and another, all walking past the door with increasing rapidity. Suraj stepped for ward but lost his balance and fell on his hands and knees. The floor beneath him was vibrating, the wheels were clattering on the rails, the carriage was swaying. The trees were running now, swooping past the train, and the telegraph poles joined them in the crazy race.

Crouching on his hands and knees, Suraj stared out of the open door and realised that the train was moving, moving fast, moving away from his home and puffing into the unknown. He crept cautiously to the door and looked out. The ground seemed to rush away from the wheels. He couldn't jump. Was there, he wondered, any way of stopping the train? He looked around the compartment again: only crates of apples. He wouldn't starve, that was one consolation.

He picked up the apple he had dropped and pulled a crate nearer to the doorway. Sitting down, he took a bite from the apple and stared out of the open door.

'Greetings, friend,' said a voice from behind, and Suraj spun round guiltily, his mouth full of apple.

A dirty, bearded face was looking out at him from behind a pile of crates. The mouth was open in a wide, paan-stained grin.

'Er—namaste,' said Suraj apprehensively. 'Who are you?'

The man stepped out from behind the crates and confronted the boy.

'I'll have one of those, too,' he said, pointing to the apple.

Suraj gave the man an apple, and stood his ground while the carriage rocked on the rails. The man took a step forward, lost his balance, and sat down on the floor.

'And where are you going, friend?' he asked. 'Have you a ticket?'

'No,' said Suraj. 'Have you?'

The man pulled at his beard and mused upon the question but did not answer it. He took a bite from the apple and said, 'No, I don't have a ticket. But I usually reserve this compartment for myself. This is the first time I've had company. Where are you going? Are you a hippy like me?'

'I don't know,' said Suraj. 'Where does this train go?'

The scruffy ticketless traveller looked concerned for a moment, then smiled and said, 'Where do you want to go?'

'I want to go everywhere,' said Suraj. 'I want to go to England and China and Africa and Greenland. I want to go all over the world!'

'Then you're on the right train,' said the man. 'This train goes everywhere. First it will take you to the sea, and there you will have to get on a ship if you want to go to China.'

'How do I get on a ship?' asked Suraj.

The man, who had been fumbling about in the folds and pockets of his shabby clothes, produced a packet of bidis and a box of matches, and began smoking the aromatic leaf.

'Can you cook?' he asked.

'Yes,' said Suraj untruthfully.

'Can you scrub a deck?'

'Why not?'

'Can you sail a ship?'

'I can sail anything.'

'Then you'll get to China,' said the man.

He leant back against a crate, stuck his dirty feet up on another crate, and puffed contentedly at his bidi.

Suraj finished his apple, took another from the crate, and dug his teeth into it. He took aim with the core of the old apple and tried to hit a telegraph pole, but missed it by metres; it wasn't the same as throwing a cricket ball. Then, to make the apple more interesting, he began to take big bites to see if he could devour it in three mouthfuls. But it took him four bites to finish the apple, so he started on another.

Suraj had always wanted to be in a train, a train that would take him to strange new places, over hundreds and hundreds of kilometres. And here was a train doing just that, and he wasn't quite sure if it was what he really wanted...

The train was coming to a station. The engine whistled, slowed down. The number of railway lines increased, crossed, spread out in different directions. Before the train could come to a stop, Suraj's companion came to the door and jumped to the ground.

'You'd better keep out of sight if you don't want to be caught!' he called. And waving his hand, he disappeared into the jungle across the railway tracks.

The train was at a siding. Suraj couldn't see any signs of life, but he heard voices and the sound of carriage doors being opened and closed. He suspected that the apples wouldn't stay in the compartment much longer, so he stuffed one into each pocket, and climbed on to a wooden rack in a corner.

Presently men's voices were heard in the doorway. Two labourers stepped into the compartment and began moving the crates towards the door, where they were taken over by others. Soon the compartment was empty.

Suraj waited until the men had gone away before coming down from the rack. After about five minutes the train started again. It shunted up and down, then gathered speed and went rushing across the plain.

Suraj felt a thrill of anticipation. Where would they be going now? He wondered what his parents would do when he failed to come home that night; they would think he had run away, or been kidnapped, or been involved in an accident. They would have the police out and there would be search parties. Suraj would be famous: the boy who disappeared!

The train came out of the jungle and passed fields of sugar-cane and villages of mud huts. Children shouted and waved to the train, though there was no one in it except Suraj, the guard and the engine-driver. Suraj waved back. Usually he was in a field, waving; today, he was actually on the train.

He was beginning to enjoy the ride. The train would take him to the sea. There would be ships with funnels and ships with sails, and there might even be one to take him across the ocean to some distant land. He felt a bit sorry for his mother and father—they *would* miss him... They would believe he had been lost for ever...! But one day, a fortune made, he would return home and then nobody would care any more about school reports and what he ate and why he came home late... Ranji would be waiting for him at the station, and Suraj would bring him back a present—an African lion, perhaps, or a transistor-radio... But he wished Ranji was with him now; he wished the ragged hippy was still with him. An adventure was always more fun when one had company.

He had finished both apples by the time the train showed signs of reaching another station. This time it seemed to be moving into the station itself, not just a siding. It passed a lot of signals and buildings and advertisement-boards before slowing to a halt beside a wide, familiar platform.

Suraj looked out of the door and caught sight of the board bearing the station's name. He was so astonished that he almost fell out of the compartment. He was back in his home town! After travelling forty or fifty kilometres, here he was, home again.

He couldn't understand it. The train hadn't turned, of that he was certain; and it hadn't been moving backwards, he was certain of that, too. He climbed out of the compartment and looked up and down the platform. Yes, the engine had changed ends! It was only the local apple train.

Suraj glowered angrily at everyone on the platform. It was as though the rest of the world had played a trick on him.

He made his way to the waiting-room and slipped into the street through the back door. He did not want a ticket-collector asking him awkward questions. It had been a free ride, and with that he comforted himself. Shrugging his shoulders, Suraj sauntered down the road to the bazaar. Some day, he thought, he'd take a train and really go somewhere; and he'd buy a ticket, just to make sure of getting there.

'I'm going everywhere,' he said fiercely. 'I'm going everywhere, and no one can stop me!'

PANTHER'S MOON

I

In the entire village, he was the first to get up. Even the dog, a big hill mastiff called Sheroo, was asleep in a corner of the dark room, curled up near the cold embers of the previous night's fire. Bisnu's tousled head emerged from his blanket. He rubbed the sleep from his eyes and sat up on his haunches. Then, gathering his wits, he crawled in the direction of the loud ticking that came from the battered little clock which occupied the second most honoured place in a niche in the wall. The most honoured place belonged to a picture of Ganesha, the god of learning, who had an elephant's head and a fat boy's body.

Bringing his face close to the clock, Bisnu could just make out the hands. It was five o'clock. He had half an hour in which to get ready and leave.

He got up, in vest and underpants, and moved quietly towards the door. The soft tread of his bare feet woke Sheroo, and the big black dog rose silently and padded behind the boy. The door opened and closed, and then the boy and the dog were outside in the early dawn. The month was June, and the nights were warm, even in the Himalayan valleys; but there was fresh dew on the grass. Bisnu felt the dew beneath his feet. He took a deep breath and began walking down to the stream.

The sound of the stream filled the small valley. At that early hour of the morning, it was the only sound; but Bisnu was hardly conscious of it. It was a sound he lived with and took for granted. It was only when he had crossed the hill, on his way to the town—and the sound of the stream grew distant—that he really began to notice it. And it was only when the stream was too far away to be heard that he really missed its sound.

He slipped out of his underclothes, gazed for a few moments at the goose pimples rising on his flesh, and then dashed into the shallow stream. As he went further in, the cold mountain water reached his loins and navel, and he gasped with shock and pleasure. He drifted slowly with the current, swam across to a small inlet which formed a fairly deep pool and plunged into the water. Sheroo hated cold water at this early hour. Had the sun been up, he would not have hesitated to join Bisnu. Now he contented himself with sitting on a smooth rock and gazing placidly at the slim brown boy splashing about in the clear water, in the widening light of dawn.

Bisnu did not stay long in the water. There wasn't time. When he returned to the house, he found his mother up, making tea and chapattis. His sister, Puja, was still asleep. She was a little older than Bisnu, a pretty girl with large black eyes, good teeth and strong arms and legs. During the day, she helped her mother in the house and in the fields. She did not go to the school with Bisnu. But when he came home in the evenings, he would try teaching her some of the things he had learnt. Their father was dead. Bisnu, at twelve, considered himself the head of the family.

He ate two chapattis, after spreading butter-oil on them. He drank a glass of hot sweet tea. His mother gave two thick chapattis to Sheroo, and the dog wolfed them down in a few minutes. Then she wrapped two chapattis and a gourd curry in some big green leaves, and handed these to Bisnu. This was his lunch packet. His mother and Puja would take their meal afterwards.

When Bisnu was dressed, he stood with folded hands before the picture of Ganesha. Ganesha is the god who blesses all beginnings. The author who begins to write a new book, the banker who opens a new ledger, the traveller who starts on a journey, all invoke the kindly help of Ganesha. And as Bisnu made a journey every day, he never left without the goodwill of the elephant-headed god.

How, one might ask, did Ganesha get his elephant's head?

When born, he was a beautiful child. Parvati, his mother, was so proud of him that she went about showing him to everyone. Unfortunately, she made the mistake of showing the child to that envious planet, Saturn, who promptly burnt off poor Ganesha's head. Parvati in despair went to Brahma, the Creator, for a new head for her son. He had no head to give her, but advised her to search for some man or animal caught in a sinful or wrong act. Parvati wandered about until she came upon an elephant sleeping with its head the wrong way, that is, to the south. She promptly removed the elephant's head and planted it on Ganesha's shoulders, where it took root.

Bisnu knew this story. He had heard it from his mother.

Wearing a white shirt and black shorts, and a pair of worn white keds, he was ready for his long walk to school, five miles up the mountain.

His sister woke up just as he was about to leave. She pushed the hair away from her face and gave Bisnu one of her rare smiles.

'I hope you have not forgotten,' she said.

'Forgotten?' said Bisnu, pretending innocence. 'Is there anything I am supposed to remember?'

'Don't tease me. You promised to buy me a pair of bangles, remember? I hope you won't spend the money on sweets, as you did last time.'

'Oh, yes, your bangles,' said Bisnu. 'Girls have nothing better to do than waste money on trinkets. Now, don't lose your temper! I'll get them for you. Red and gold are the colours you want?'

'Yes, Brother,' said Puja gently, pleased that Bisnu had remembered the colours. 'And for your dinner tonight we'll make you something special. Won't we, Mother?'

'Yes. But hurry up and dress. There is some ploughing to be done today. The rains will soon be here, if the gods are kind.'

'The monsoon will be late this year,' said Bisnu. 'Mr Nautiyal, our teacher, told us so. He said it had nothing to do with the gods.'

'Be off, you are getting late,' said Puja, before Bisnu could begin an argument with his mother. She was diligently winding the old clock. It was quite light in the room. The sun would be up any minute.

Bisnu shouldered his school bag, kissed his mother, pinched his sister's cheeks and left the house. He started climbing the steep path up the mountainside. Sheroo bounded ahead; for he, too, always went with Bisnu to school.

Five miles to school. Every day, except Sunday, Bisnu walked five miles to school; and in the evening, he walked home again. There was no school in his own small village of Manjari, for the village consisted of only five families. The nearest school was at Kemptee, a small township on the bus route through the district of Garhwal. A number of boys walked to school, from distances of two or three miles; their villages were not quite as remote as Manjari. But Bisnu's village lay right at the bottom of the mountain, a drop of over two thousand feet from Kemptee. There was no proper road between the village and the town.

In Kemptee there was a school, a small mission hospital, a post office and several shops. In Manjari village there were none of these amenities. If you were sick, you stayed at home until you got well; if you were very sick, you walked or were carried to the hospital, up the five mile path. If you wanted to buy something, you went without it; but if you wanted it very badly, you could walk the five miles to Kemptee.

Manjari was known as the Five Mile Village.

Twice a week, if there were any letters, a postman came to the village. Bisnu usually passed the postman on his way to and from school.

There were other boys in Manjari village, but Bisnu was the only one who went to school. His mother would not have fussed if he had stayed at home and worked in the fields. That was what the other boys did; all except lazy Chittru, who preferred fishing in the stream or helping himself to the fruit of other people's trees. But Bisnu went to school. He went because he wanted to. No one could force him to go; and no one could stop him from going. He had set his heart on receiving a good schooling. He wanted to read and write as well as anyone in the big world, the world that seemed to begin only where the mountains ended. He felt cut off from the world in his small valley. He would rather live at the top of a mountain than at the bottom of one. That was why he liked climbing to Kemptee, it took him to the top of the mountain; and from its ridge he could look down on his own valley to the north, and on the wide endless plains stretching towards the south.

The plainsman looks to the hills for the needs of his spirit but the hill man looks to the plains for a living.

Leaving the village and the fields below him, Bisnu climbed steadily up the bare hillside, now dry and brown. By the time the sun was up, he had entered the welcome shade of an oak and rhododendron forest. Sheroo went bounding ahead, chasing squirrels and barking at langoors.

A colony of langoors lived in the oak forest. They fed on oak leaves, acorns and other green things, and usually remained in the trees, coming down to the ground only to play or bask in the sun. They were beautiful, supple-limbed animals, with black faces and silver-grey coats and long, sensitive tails. They leapt from tree to tree with great agility. The young ones wrestled on the grass like boys.

A dignified community, the langoors did not have the cheekiness or dishonest habits of the red monkeys of the plains; they did not approach dogs or humans. But they had grown used to Bisnu's comings and goings, and did not fear him. Some of the older ones would watch him quietly, a little puzzled. They did not go near the town, because the Kemptee boys threw stones at them. And anyway, the oak forest gave them all the food they required.

Emerging from the trees, Bisnu crossed a small brook. Here he stopped to drink the fresh clean water of a spring. The brook tumbled down the mountain and joined the river a little below Bisnu's village. Coming from another direction was a second path, and at the junction of the two paths Sarru was waiting for him.

Sarru came from a small village about three miles from Bisnu's and closer to the town. He had two large milk cans slung over his shoulders. Every morning he carried this milk to town, selling one can to the school and the other to Mrs Taylor, the lady doctor at the small mission hospital. He was a little older than Bisnu but not as well-built.

They hailed each other, and Sarru fell into step beside Bisnu. They often met at this spot, keeping each other company for the remaining two miles to Kemptee.

'There was a panther in our village last night,' said Sarru.

This information interested but did not excite Bisnu. Panthers were common enough in the hills and did not usually present a problem except during the winter months, when their natural prey was scarce. Then, occasionally, a panther would take to haunting the outskirts of a village, seizing a careless dog or a stray goat.

'Did you lose any animals?' asked Bisnu.

'No. It tried to get into the cowshed but the dogs set up an alarm. We drove it off.'

'It must be the same one which came around last winter. We lost a calf and two dogs in our village.'

'Wasn't that the one the shikaris wounded? I hope it hasn't become a cattle lifter.'

'It could be the same. It has a bullet in its leg. These hunters are the people who cause all the trouble. They think it's easy to shoot a panther. It would be better if they missed altogether, but they usually wound it.'

'And then the panther's too slow to catch the barking deer, and starts on our own animals.'

'We're lucky it didn't become a man-eater. Do you

remember the man-eater six years ago? I was very small then. My father told me all about it. Ten people were killed in our valley alone. What happened to it?'

'I don't know. Some say it poisoned itself when it ate the headman of another village.'

Bisnu laughed. 'No one liked that old villain. He must have been a man-eater himself in some previous existence!' They linked arms and scrambled up the stony path. Sheroo began barking and ran ahead. Someone was coming down the path.

It was Mela Ram, the postman.

II

'Any letters for us?' asked Bisnu and Sarru together.

They never received any letters but that did not stop them from asking. It was one way of finding out who had received letters.

'You're welcome to all of them,' said Mela Ram, 'if you'll carry my bag for me.'

'Not today,' said Sarru. 'We're busy today. Is there a letter from Corporal Ghanshyam for his family?'

'Yes, there is a postcard for his people. He is posted on the Ladakh border now and finds it very cold there.'

Postcards, unlike sealed letters, were considered public property and were read by everyone. The senders knew that too, and so Corporal Ghanshyam Singh was careful to mention that he expected a promotion very soon. He wanted everyone in his village to know it.

Mela Ram, complaining of sore feet, continued on his way, and the boys carried on up the path. It was eight o'clock when they reached Kemptee. Dr Taylor's outpatients were just beginning to trickle in at the hospital gate. The doctor was trying to prop up a rose creeper which had blown down during the night. She liked attending to her plants in the mornings, before starting on her patients. She found this helped her in her work. There was a lot in common between ailing plants and ailing people.

Dr Taylor was fifty, white-haired but fresh in the face and full of vitality. She had been in India for twenty years, and ten of these had been spent working in the hill regions.

She saw Bisnu coming down the road. She knew about the boy and his long walk to school and admired him for his keenness and sense of purpose. She wished there were more like him.

Bisnu greeted her shyly. Sheroo barked and put his paws up on the gate.

'Yes, there's a bone for you,' said Dr Taylor. She often put aside bones for the big black dog, for she knew that Bisnu's people could not afford to give the dog a regular diet of meat—though he did well enough on milk and chapattis.

She threw the bone over the gate and Sheroo caught it before it fell. The school bell began ringing and Bisnu broke into a run. Sheroo loped along behind the boy.

When Bisnu entered the school gate, Sheroo sat down on the grass of the compound. He would remain there until the lunchbreak. He knew of various ways of amusing himself during school hours and had friends among the bazaar dogs. But just then he didn't want company. He had his bone to get on with.

Mr Nautiyal, Bisnu's teacher, was in a bad mood. He was a keen rose grower and only that morning, on getting up and looking out of his bedroom window, he had been horrified to see a herd of goats in his garden. He had chased them down the road with a stick but the damage had already been done. His prize roses had all been consumed.

Mr Nautiyal had been so upset that he had gone without his breakfast. He had also cut himself whilst shaving. Thus, his mood had gone from bad to worse. Several times during the day, he brought down his ruler on the knuckles of any boy who irritated him. Bisnu was one of his best pupils. But even Bisnu irritated him by asking too many questions about a new sum which Mr Nautiyal didn't feel like explaining.

That was the kind of day it was for Mr Nautiyal. Most school teachers know similar days.

'Poor Mr Nautiyal,' thought Bisnu. 'I wonder why he's so upset. It must be because of his pay. He doesn't get much money. But he's a good teacher. I hope he doesn't take another job.'

But after Mr Nautiyal had eaten his lunch, his mood improved (as it always did after a meal), and the rest of the day passed serenely. Armed with a bundle of homework, Bisnu came out from the school compound at four o'clock, and was immediately joined by Sheroo. He proceeded down the road in the company of several of his classfellows. But he did not linger long in the bazaar. There were five miles to walk, and he did not like to get home too late. Usually, he reached his house just as it was beginning to get dark.

Sarru had gone home long ago, and Bisnu had to make the return journey on his own. It was a good opportunity to memorize the words of an English poem he had been asked to learn.

Bisnu had reached the little brook when he remembered the bangles he had promised to buy for his sister.

'Oh, I've forgotten them again,' he said aloud. 'Now I'll catch it—and she's probably made something special for my dinner!'

Sheroo, to whom these words were addressed, paid no attention but bounded off into the oak forest. Bisnu looked around for the monkeys but they were nowhere to be seen.

'Strange,' he thought, 'I wonder why they have disappeared.'

He was startled by a sudden sharp cry, followed by a fierce yelp. He knew at once that Sheroo was in trouble. The noise came from the bushes down the khud, into which the dog had rushed but a few seconds previously.

Bisnu jumped off the path and ran down the slope towards the bushes. There was no dog and not a sound. He whistled and called, but there was no response. Then he saw something lying on the dry grass. He picked it up. It was a portion of a dog's collar, stained with blood. It was Sheroo's collar and Sheroo's blood.

Bisnu did not search further. He knew, without a doubt, that Sheroo had been seized by a panther. No other animal could have attacked so silently and swiftly and carried off a big dog without a struggle. Sheroo was dead—must have been dead within seconds of being caught and flung into the air. Bisnu knew the danger that lay in wait for him if he followed the blood trail through the trees. The panther would attack anyone who interfered with its meal.

With tears starting in his eyes, Bisnu carried on down the path to the village. His fingers still clutched the little bit of bloodstained collar that was all that was left to him of his dog.

III

Bisnu was not a very sentimental boy, but he sorrowed for his dog who had been his companion on many a hike into the hills and forests. He did not sleep that night, but turned restlessly from side to side moaning softly. After some time he felt Puja's hand on his head. She began stroking his brow. He took her hand in his own and the clasp of her rough, warm familiar hand gave him a feeling of comfort and security.

Next morning, when he went down to the stream to bathe, he missed the presence of his dog. He did not stay long in the water. It wasn't as much fun when there was no Sheroo to watch him.

When Bisnu's mother gave him his food, she told him to be careful and hurry home that evening. A panther, even if it is only a cowardly lifter of sheep or dogs, is not to be trifled with. And this particular panther had shown some daring by seizing the dog even before it was dark.

Still, there was no question of staying away from school. If Bisnu remained at home every time a panther put in an appearance, he might as well stop going to school altogether.

He set off even earlier than usual and reached the meeting of the paths long before Sarru. He did not wait for his friend, because he did not feel like talking about the loss of his dog. It was not the day for the postman, and so Bisnu reached Kemptee without meeting anyone on the way. He tried creeping past the hospital gate unnoticed, but Dr Taylor saw him and the first thing she said was: 'Where's Sheroo? I've got something for him.'

When Dr Taylor saw the boy's face, she knew at once that something was wrong.

'What is it, Bisnu?' she asked. She looked quickly up and down the road. 'Is it Sheroo?'

He nodded gravely.

'A panther took him,' he said.

'In the village?'

'No, while we were walking home through the forest. I did

not see anything—but I heard.'

Dr Taylor knew that there was nothing she could say that would console him, and she tried to conceal the bone which she had brought out for the dog, but Bisnu noticed her hiding it behind her back and the tears welled up in his eyes. He turned away and began running down the road.

His schoolfellows noticed Sheroo's absence and questioned Bisnu. He had to tell them everything. They were full of sympathy, but they were also quite thrilled at what had happened and kept pestering Bisnu for all the details. There was a lot of noise in the classroom, and Mr Nautiyal had to call for order. When he learnt what had happened, he patted Bisnu on the head and told him that he need not attend school for the rest of the day. But Bisnu did not want to go home. After school, he got into a fight with one of the boys, and that helped him forget.

IV

The panther that plunged the village into an atmosphere of gloom and terror may not have been the same panther that took Sheroo. There was no way of knowing, and it would have made no difference, because the panther that came by night and struck at the people of Manjari was that most feared of wild creatures, a man-eater.

Nine-year-old Sanjay, son of Kalam Singh, was the first child to be attacked by the panther.

Kalam Singh's house was the last in the village and nearest the stream. Like the other houses, it was quite small, just a room above and a stable below, with steps leading up from outside the house. He lived there with his wife, two sons (Sanjay was the youngest) and little daughter Basanti who had just turned three.

Sanjay had brought his father's cows home after grazing them on the hillside in the company of other children. He had also brought home an edible wild plant, which his mother cooked into a tasty dish for their evening meal. They had their food at dusk, sitting on the floor of their single room, and soon after, settled down for the night. Sanjay curled up in his favourite spot, with his head near the door, where he got a little fresh air. As the nights were warm, the door was usually left a little ajar. Sanjay's mother piled ash on the embers of the fire and the family was soon asleep.

No one heard the stealthy padding of a panther approaching the door, pushing it wide open. But suddenly there were sounds of a frantic struggle, and Sanjay's stifled cries were mixed with the grunts of the panther. Kalam Singh leapt to his feet with a shout. The panther had dragged Sanjay out of the door and was pulling him down the steps, when Kalam Singh started battering at the animal with a large stone. The rest of the family screamed in terror, rousing the entire village. A number of men came to Kalam Singh's assistance, and the panther was driven off. But Sanjay lay unconscious.

Someone brought a lantern and the boy's mother screamed when she saw her small son with his head lying in a pool of blood. It looked as if the side of his head had been eaten off by the panther. But he was still alive, and as Kalam Singh plastered ash on the boy's head to stop the bleeding, he found that though the scalp had been torn off one side of the head, the bare bone was smooth and unbroken.

'He won't live through the night,' said a neighbour. 'We'll have to carry him down to the river in the morning.'

The dead were always cremated on the banks of a small river which flowed past Manjari village.

Suddenly the panther, still prowling about the village, called out in rage and frustration, and the villagers rushed to their homes in panic and barricaded themselves in for the night.

Sanjay's mother sat by the boy for the rest of the night, weeping and watching. Towards dawn he started to moan and show signs of coming round. At this sign of returning consciousness, Kalam Singh rose determinedly and looked around for his stick.

He told his elder son to remain behind with the mother and daughter, as he was going to take Sanjay to Dr Taylor at the hospital.

'See, he is moaning and in pain,' said Kalam Singh. 'That means he has a chance to live if he can be treated at once.'

With a stout stick in his hand, and Sanjay on his back, Kalam Singh set off on the two miles of hard mountain track to the hospital at Kemptee. His son, a bloodstained cloth around his head, was moaning but still unconscious. When at last Kalam Singh climbed up through the last fields below the hospital, he asked for the doctor and stammered out an account of what had happened.

It was a terrible injury, as Dr Taylor discovered. The bone over almost one-third of the head was bare and the scalp was torn all round. As the father told his story, the doctor cleaned and dressed the wound, and then gave Sanjay a shot of penicillin to prevent sepsis. Later, Kalam Singh carried the boy home again.

V

After this, the panther went away for some time. But the people of Manjari could not be sure of its whereabouts. They kept to their houses after dark and shut their doors. Bisnu had to stop going to school, because there was no one to accompany him and it was dangerous to go alone. This worried him, because his final exam was only a few weeks off and he would be missing important classwork. When he wasn't in the fields, helping with the sowing of rice and maize, he would be sitting in the shade of a chestnut tree, going through his well-thumbed second-hand school books. He had no other reading, except for a copy of the Ramayana and a Hindi translation of *Alice's Adventures in Wonderland*. These were well-preserved, read only in fits and starts, and usually kept locked in his mother's old tin trunk.

Sanjay had nightmares for several nights and woke up screaming. But with the resilience of youth, he quickly recovered. At the end of the week he was able to walk to the hospital, though his father always accompanied him. Even a desperate panther will hesitate to attack a party of two. Sanjay, with his thin little face and huge bandaged head, looked a pathetic figure, but he was getting better and the wound looked healthy.

Bisnu often went to see him, and the two boys spent long hours together near the stream. Sometimes Chittru would join them, and they would try catching fish with a home-made net. They were often successful in taking home one or two mountain trout. Sometimes, Bisnu and Chittru wrestled in the shallow water or on the grassy banks of the stream. Chittru was a chubby boy with a broad chest, strong legs and thighs, and when he used his weight he got Bisnu under him. But Bisnu was hard and wiry and had very strong wrists and fingers. When he had Chittru in a vice, the bigger boy would cry out and give up the struggle. Sanjay could not join in these games.

He had never been a very strong boy and he needed plenty of rest if his wounds were to heal well.

The panther had not been seen for over a week, and the

people of Manjari were beginning to hope that it might have moved on over the mountain or further down the valley.

'I think I can start going to school again,' said Bisnu. 'The panther has gone away.'

'Don't be too sure,' said Puja. 'The moon is full these days and perhaps it is only being cautious.'

'Wait a few days,' said their mother. 'It is better to wait. Perhaps you could go the day after tomorrow when Sanjay goes to the hospital with his father. Then you will not be alone.'

And so, two days later, Bisnu went up to Kemptee with Sanjay and Kalam Singh. Sanjay's wound had almost healed over. Little islets of flesh had grown over the bone. Dr Taylor told him that he need come to see her only once a fortnight, instead of every third day.

Bisnu went to his school, and was given a warm welcome by his friends and by Mr Nautiyal.

'You'll have to work hard,' said his teacher. 'You have to catch up with the others. If you like, I can give you some extra time after classes.'

'Thank you, sir, but it will make me late,' said Bisnu. 'I must get home before it is dark, otherwise my mother will worry. I think the panther has gone but nothing is certain.'

'Well, you mustn't take risks. Do your best, Bisnu. Work hard and you'll soon catch up with your lessons.'

Sanjay and Kalam Singh were waiting for him outside the school. Together they took the path down to Manjari, passing the postman on the way. Mela Ram said he had heard that the panther was in another district and that there was nothing to fear. He was on his rounds again.

Nothing happened on the way. The langoors were back in their favourite part of the forest. Bisnu got home just as the kerosene lamp was being lit. Puja met him at the door with a winsome smile.

'Did you get the bangles?' she asked.

But Bisnu had forgotten again.

VI

There had been a thunderstorm and some rain—a short, sharp shower which gave the villagers hope that the monsoon would arrive on time. It brought out the thunder lilies—pink, crocus-like flowers which sprang up on the hillsides immediately after a summer shower.

Bisnu, on his way home from school, was caught in the rain. He knew the shower would not last, so he took shelter in a small cave and, to pass the time, began doing sums, scratching figures in the damp earth with the end of a stick.

When the rain stopped, he came out from the cave and continued down the path. He wasn't in a hurry. The rain had made everything smell fresh and good. The scent from fallen pine needles rose from wet earth. The leaves of the oak trees had been washed clean and a light breeze turned them about, showing their silver undersides. The birds, refreshed and high-spirited, set up a terrific noise. The worst offenders were the yellow-bottomed bulbuls who squabbled and fought in the blackberry bushes. A barbet, high up in the branches of a deodar, set up its querulous, plaintive call. And a flock of bright green parrots came swooping down the hill to settle in a wild plum tree and feast on the unripe fruit. The langoors, too, had been revived by the rain. They leapt friskily from tree to tree greeting Bisnu with little grunts.

He was almost out of the oak forest when he heard a

faint bleating. Presently, a little goat came stumbling up the path towards him. The kid was far from home and must have strayed from the rest of the herd. But it was not yet conscious of being lost. It came to Bisnu with a hop, skip and a jump and started nuzzling against his legs like a cat.

'I wonder who you belong to,' mused Bisnu, stroking the little creature. 'You'd better come home with me until someone claims you.'

He didn't have to take the kid in his arms. It was used to humans and followed close at his heels. Now that darkness was coming on, Bisnu walked a little faster.

He had not gone very far when he heard the sawing grunt of a panther.

The sound came from the hill to the right, and Bisnu judged the distance to be anything from 100 to 200 yards. He hesitated on the path, wondering what to do. Then he picked the kid up in his arms and hurried on in the direction of home and safety.

The panther called again, much closer now. If it was an ordinary panther, it would go away on finding that the kid was with Bisnu. If it was the man-eater, it would not hesitate to attack the boy, for no man-eater fears a human. There was no time to lose and there did not seem much point in running. Bisnu looked up and down the hillside. The forest was far behind him and there were only a few trees in his vicinity. He chose a spruce.

The branches of the Himalayan spruce are very brittle and snap easily beneath a heavy weight. They were strong enough to support Bisnu's light frame. It was unlikely they would take the weight of a full-grown panther. At least that was what Bisnu hoped.

Holding the kid with one arm, Bisnu gripped a low branch

and swung himself up into the tree. He was a good climber. Slowly but confidently he climbed halfway up the tree, until he was about twelve feet above the ground. He couldn't go any higher without risking a fall.

He had barely settled himself in the crook of a branch when the panther came into the open, running into the clearing at a brisk trot. This was no stealthy approach, no wary stalking of its prey. It was the man-eater, all right. Bisnu felt a cold shiver run down his spine. He felt a little sick.

The panther stood in the clearing with a slight thrusting forward of the head. This gave it the appearance of gazing intently and rather short-sightedly at some invisible object in the clearing. But there is nothing short-sighted about a panther's vision. Its sight and hearing are acute.

Bisnu remained motionless in the tree and sent up a prayer to all the gods he could think of. But the kid began bleating. The panther looked up and gave its deep-throated, rasping grunt—a fearsome sound, calculated to strike terror in any treeborne animal. Many a monkey, petrified by a panther's roar, has fallen from its perch to make a meal for Mr Spots. The man-eater was trying the same technique on Bisnu. But though the boy was trembling with fright, he clung firmly to the base of the spruce tree.

The panther did not make any attempt to leap into the tree. Perhaps, it knew instinctively that this was not the type of tree that it could climb. Instead, it described a semicircle round the tree, keeping its face turned towards Bisnu. Then it disappeared into the bushes.

The man-eater was cunning. It hoped to put the boy off his guard, perhaps entice him down from the tree. For, a few seconds later, with a half-humorous growl, it rushed back into the clearing and then stopped, staring up at the boy in some surprise. The panther was getting frustrated. It snarled, and putting its forefeet up against the tree trunk began scratching at the bark in the manner of an ordinary domestic cat. The tree shook at each thud of the beast's paw.

Bisnu began shouting for help.

The moon had not yet come up. Down in Manjari village, Bisnu's mother and sister stood in their lighted doorway, gazing anxiously up the pathway. Every now and then, Puja would turn to take a look at the small clock.

Sanjay's father appeared in a field below. He had a kerosene lantern in his hand.

'Sister, isn't your boy home as yet?' he asked.

'No, he hasn't arrived. We are very worried. He should have been home an hour ago. Do you think the panther will be about tonight? There's going to be a moon.'

'True, but it will be dark for another hour. I will fetch the other menfolk, and we will go up the mountain for your boy. There may have been a landslide during the rain. Perhaps the path has been washed away.'

'Thank you, brother. But arm yourselves, just in case the panther is about.'

'I will take my spear,' said Kalam Singh. 'I have sworn to spear that devil when I find him. There is some evil spirit dwelling in the beast and it must be destroyed!'

'I am coming with you,' said Puja.

'No, you cannot go,' said her mother. 'It's bad enough that Bisnu is in danger. You stay at home with me. This is work for men.'

'I shall be safe with them,' insisted Puja. 'I am going, Mother!' And she jumped down the embankment into the field and followed Sanjay's father through the village.

Ten minutes later, two men armed with axes had joined Kalam Singh in the courtyard of his house, and the small party moved silently and swiftly up the mountain path. Puja walked in the middle of the group, holding the lantern. As soon as the village lights were hidden by a shoulder of the hill, the men began to shout—both to frighten the panther, if it was about, and to give themselves courage.

Bisnu's mother closed the front door and turned to the image of Ganesha, the god for comfort and help.

Bisnu's calls were carried on the wind, and Puja and the men heard him while they were still half a mile away. Their own shouts increased in volume and, hearing their voices, Bisnu felt strength return to his shaking limbs. Emboldened by the approach of his own people, he began shouting insults at the snarling panther, then throwing twigs and small branches at the enraged animal. The kid added its bleats to the boy's shouts, the birds took up the chorus. The langoors squealed and grunted, the searchers shouted themselves hoarse, and the panther howled with rage. The forest had never before been so noisy.

As the search party drew near, they could hear the panther's savage snarls, and hurried, fearing that perhaps Bisnu had been seized. Puja began to run.

'Don't rush ahead, girl,' said Kalam Singh. 'Stay between us.'

The panther, now aware of the approaching humans, stood still in the middle of the clearing, head thrust forward in a familiar stance. There seemed too many men for one panther. When the animal saw the light of the lantern dancing between the trees, it turned, snarled defiance and hate, and without another look at the boy in the tree, disappeared into the bushes. It was not yet ready for a showdown.

VII

Nobody turned up to claim the little goat, so Bisnu kept it. A goat was a poor substitute for a dog, but, like Mary's lamb, it followed Bisnu wherever he went, and the boy couldn't help being touched by its devotion. He took it down to the stream, where it would skip about in the shallows and nibble the sweet grass that grew on the banks.

As for the panther, frustrated in its attempt on Bisnu's life, it did not wait long before attacking another human.

It was Chittru who came running down the path one afternoon, bubbling excitedly about the panther and the postman.

Chittru, deeming it safe to gather ripe bilberries in the daytime, had walked about half a mile up the path from the village, when he had stumbled across Mela Ram's mailbag lying on the ground. Of the postman himself there was no sign. But a trail of blood led through the bushes.

Once again, a party of men headed by Kalam Singh and accompanied by Bisnu and Chittru, went out to look for the postman. But though they found Mela Ram's bloodstained clothes, they could not find his body. The panther had made no mistake this time.

It was to be several weeks before Manjari had a new postman.

A few days after Mela Ram's disappearance, an old woman was sleeping with her head near the open door of her house. She had been advised to sleep inside with the door closed, but the nights were hot and anyway the old woman was a little deaf, and in the middle of the night, an hour before moonrise, the panther seized her by the throat. Her strangled cry woke her grown-up son, and all the men in the village woke up at his shouts and came running.

The panther dragged the old woman out of the house and down the steps, but left her when the men approached with their axes and spears, and made off into the bushes. The old woman was still alive, and the men made a rough stretcher of bamboo and vines and started carrying her up the path. But they had not gone far when she began to cough, and because of her terrible throat wounds, her lungs collapsed and she died.

It was the 'dark of the month'—the week of the new moon when nights are darkest.

Bisnu, closing the front door and lighting the kerosene lantern, said, 'I wonder where that panther is tonight!'

The panther was busy in another village: Sarru's village.

A woman and her daughter had been out in the evening bedding the cattle down in the stable. The girl had gone into the house and the woman was following. As she bent down to go in at the low door, the panther sprang from the bushes. Fortunately, one of its paws hit the doorpost and broke the force of the attack, or the woman would have been killed. When she cried out, the men came round shouting and the panther slunk off. The woman had deep scratches on her back and was badly shocked.

The next day, a small party of villagers presented themselves in front of the magistrate's office at Kemptee and demanded that something be done about the panther. But the magistrate was away on tour, and there was no one else in Kemptee who had a gun. Mr Nautiyal met the villagers and promised to write to a well-known shikari, but said that it would be at least a fortnight before the shikari would be able to come.

Bisnu was fretting because he could not go to school. Most

boys would be only too happy to miss school, but when you are living in a remote village in the mountains and having an education is the only way of seeing the world, you look forward to going to school, even if it is five miles from home. Bisnu's exams were only two weeks off, and he didn't want to remain in the same class while the others were promoted. Besides, he knew he could pass even though he had missed a number of lessons. But he had to sit for the exams. He couldn't miss them.

'Cheer up, Bhaiya,' said Puja, as they sat drinking glasses of hot tea after their evening meal. 'The panther may go away once the rains break.'

'Even the rains are late this year,' said Bisnu. 'It's so hot and dry. Can't we open the door?'

'And be dragged down the steps by the panther?' said his mother. 'It isn't safe to have the window open, let alone the door.' And she went to the small window—through which a cat would have found difficulty in passing—and bolted it firmly.

With a sigh of resignation, Bisnu threw off all his clothes except his underwear and stretched himself out on the earthen floor.

'We will be rid of the beast soon,' said his mother. 'I know it in my heart. Our prayers will be heard, and you shall go to school and pass your exams.'

To cheer up her children, she told them a humorous story which had been handed down to her by her grandmother. It was all about a tiger, a panther and a bear, the three of whom were made to feel very foolish by a thief hiding in the hollow trunk of a banyan tree. Bisnu was sleepy and did not listen very attentively. He dropped off to sleep before the story was finished.

When he woke, it was dark and his mother and sister were asleep on the cot. He wondered what it was that had woken him. He could hear his sister's easy breathing and the steady ticking of the clock. Far away an owl hooted—an unlucky sign, his mother would have said; but she was asleep and Bisnu was not superstitious.

And then he heard something scratching at the door, and the hair on his head felt tight and prickly. It was like a cat scratching, only louder. The door creaked a little whenever it felt the impact of the paw—a heavy paw, as Bisnu could tell from the dull sound it made.

'It's the panther,' he muttered under his breath, sitting up on the hard floor.

The door, he felt, was strong enough to resist the panther's weight. And if he set up an alarm, he could rouse the village. But the middle of the night was no time for the bravest of men to tackle a panther.

In a corner of the room stood a long bamboo stick with a sharp knife tied to one end, which Bisnu sometimes used for spearing fish. Crawling on all fours across the room, he grasped the home-made spear, and then scrambling on to a cupboard, he drew level with the skylight window. He could get his head and shoulders through the window.

'What are you doing up there?' said Puja, who had woken up at the sound of Bisnu shuffling about the room.

'Be quiet,' said Bisnu. 'You'll wake Mother.'

Their mother was awake by now. 'Come down from there, Bisnu. I can hear a noise outside.'

'Don't worry,' said Bisnu, who found himself looking down on the wriggling animal which was trying to get its paw in under the door. With his mother and Puja awake, there was no time to lose. He had got the spear through the window, and though he could not manoeuvre it so as to strike the panther's head, he brought the sharp end down with considerable force on the animal's rump.

With a roar of pain and rage the man-eater leapt down from the steps and disappeared into the darkness. It did not pause to see what had struck it. Certain that no human could have come upon it in that fashion, it ran fearfully to its lair, howling until the pain subsided.

VIII

A panther is an enigma. There are occasions when it proves himself to be the most cunning animal under the sun, and yet the very next day it will walk into an obvious trap that no self-respecting jackal would ever go near. One day a panther will prove itself to be a complete coward and run like a hare from a couple of dogs, and the very next it will dash in amongst half a dozen men sitting round a camp fire and inflict terrible injuries on them.

It is not often that a panther is taken by surprise, as its power of sight and hearing are very acute. It is a master at the art of camouflage, and its spotted coat is admirably suited for the purpose. It does not need heavy jungle to hide in. A couple of bushes and the light and shade from surrounding trees are enough to make it almost invisible.

Because the Manjari panther had been fooled by Bisnu, it did not mean that it was a stupid panther. It simply meant that it had been a little careless. And Bisnu and Puja, growing in confidence since their midnight encounter with the animal, became a little careless themselves.

Puja was hoeing the last field above the house and Bisnu, at the other end of the same field, was chopping up several branches of green oak, prior to leaving the wood to dry in the loft. It was late afternoon and the descending sun glinted in patches on the small river. It was a time of day when only the most desperate and daring of man-eaters would be likely to show itself.

Pausing for a moment to wipe the sweat from his brow, Bisnu glanced up at the hillside, and his eye caught sight of a rock on the brown of the hill which seemed unfamiliar to him. Just as he was about to look elsewhere, the round rock began to grow and then alter its shape, and Bisnu watching in fascination was at last able to make out the head and forequarters of the panther. It looked enormous from the angle at which he saw it, and for a moment he thought it was a tiger. But Bisnu knew instinctively that it was the man-eater.

Slowly, the wary beast pulled itself to its feet and began to walk round the side of the great rock. For a second it disappeared and Bisnu wondered if it had gone away. Then it reappeared and the boy was all excitement again. Very slowly and silently the panther walked across the face of the rock until it was in direct line with the corner of the field where Puja was working.

With a thrill of horror Bisnu realised that the panther was stalking his sister. He shook himself free from the spell which had woven itself round him and shouting hoarsely ran forward.

'Run, Puja, run!' he called. 'It's on the hill above you!'

Puja turned to see what Bisnu was shouting about. She saw him gesticulate to the hill behind her, looked up just in time to see the panther crouching for his spring.

With great presence of mind, she leapt down the banking of the field and tumbled into an irrigation ditch.

The springing panther missed its prey, lost its foothold on the slippery shale banking and somersaulted into the ditch a few feet away from Puja. Before the animal could recover from its surprise, Bisnu was dashing down the slope, swinging his axe and shouting, '*Maro, maro!* (Kill, kill!)'

Two men came running across the field. They, too, were armed with axes. Together with Bisnu they made a half-circle around the snarling animal, which turned at bay and plunged at them in order to get away. Puja wriggled along the ditch on her stomach. The men aimed their axes at the panther's head, and Bisnu had the satisfaction of getting in a well-aimed blow between the eyes. The animal then charged straight at one of the men, knocked him over and tried to get at his throat. Just then Sanjay's father arrived with his long spear. He plunged the end of the spear into the panther's neck.

The panther left its victim and ran into the bushes, dragging the spear through the grass and leaving a trail of blood on the ground. The men followed cautiously—all except the man who had been wounded and who lay on the ground, while Puja and the other womenfolk rushed up to help him.

The panther had made for the bed of the stream and Bisnu, Sanjay's father and their companion were able to follow it quite easily. The water was red where the panther had crossed the stream, and the rocks were stained with blood. After they had gone downstream for about a furlong, they found the panther lying still on its side at the edge of the water. It was mortally wounded, but it continued to wave its tail like an angry cat. Then, even the tail lay still.

'It is dead,' said Bisnu. 'It will not trouble us again in this body.'

'Let us be certain,' said Sanjay's father, and he bent down and pulled the panther's tail.

There was no response.

'It is dead,' said Kalam Singh. 'No panther would suffer such an insult were it alive!'

They cut down a long piece of thick bamboo and tied the panther to it by its feet. Then, with their enemy hanging upside down from the bamboo pole, they started back for the village.

'There will be a feast at my house tonight,' said Kalam Singh. 'Everyone in the village must come. And tomorrow we will visit all the villages in the valley and show them the dead panther, so that they may move about again without fear.'

'We can sell the skin in Kemptee,' said their companion. 'It will fetch a good price.'

'But the claws we will give to Bisnu,' said Kalam Singh, putting his arm around the boy's shoulders. 'He has done a man's work today. He deserves the claws.'

A panther's or tiger's claws are considered to be lucky charms.

'I will take only three claws,' said Bisnu. 'One each for my mother and sister, and one for myself. You may give the others to Sanjay and Chittru and the smaller children.'

As the sun set, a big fire was lit in the middle of the village of Manjari and the people gathered round it, singing and laughing. Kalam Singh killed his fattest goat and there was meat for everyone.

IX

Bisnu was on his way home. He had just handed in his first paper, arithmetic, which he had found quite easy. Tomorrow it would be algebra, and when he got home he would have to practice square roots and cube roots and fractional coefficients.

Mr Nautiyal and the entire class had been happy that he

had been able to sit for the exams. He was also a hero to them for his part in killing the panther. The story had spread through the villages with the rapidity of a forest fire, a fire which was now raging in Kemptee town.

When he walked past the hospital, he was whistling cheerfully. Dr Taylor waved to him from the veranda steps.

'How is Sanjay now?' she asked.

'He is well,' said Bisnu.

'And your mother and sister?'

'They are well,' said Bisnu.

'Are you going to get yourself a new dog?'

'I am thinking about it,' said Bisnu. 'At present I have a baby goat—I am teaching it to swim!'

He started down the path to the valley. Dark clouds had gathered and there was a rumble of thunder. A storm was imminent.

'Wait for me!' shouted Sarru, running down the path behind Bisnu, his milk pails clanging against each other. He fell into step beside Bisnu.

'Well, I hope we don't have any more man-eaters for some time,' he said. 'I've lost a lot of money by not being able to take milk up to Kemptee.'

'We should be safe as long as a shikari doesn't wound another panther. There was an old bullet wound in the man-eater's thigh. That's why it couldn't hunt in the forest. The deer were too fast for it.'

'Is there a new postman yet?'

'He starts tomorrow. A cousin of Mela Ram's.'

When they reached the parting of their ways it had begun to rain a little.

'I must hurry,' said Sarru. 'It's going to get heavier any

minute.' 'I feel like getting wet,' said Bisnu. This time it's the monsoon, I'm sure.'

Bisnu entered the forest on his own, and at the same time the rain came down in heavy opaque sheets. The trees shook in the wind, the langoors chattered with excitement.

It was still pouring when Bisnu emerged from the forest, drenched to the skin. But the rain stopped suddenly, just as the village of Manjari came in view. The sun appeared through a rift in the clouds. The leaves and the grass gave out a sweet, fresh smell.

Bisnu could see his mother and sister in the field transplanting the rice seedlings. The menfolk were driving the yoked oxen through the thin mud of the fields, while the children hung on to the oxen's tails, standing on the plain wooden harrows and with weird cries and shouts sending the animals almost at a gallop along the narrow terraces.

Bisnu felt the urge to be with them, working in the fields. He ran down the path, his feet falling softly on the wet earth. Puja saw him coming and waved to him. She met him at the edge of the field.

'How did you find your paper today?' she asked.

'Oh, it was easy.' Bisnu slipped his hand into hers and together they walked across the field. Puja felt something smooth and hard against her fingers, and before she could see what Bisnu was doing, he had slipped a pair of bangles over her wrist.

'I remembered,' he said, with a sense of achievement. Puja looked at the bangles and burst out: 'But they are blue, Bhai, and I wanted red and gold bangles!' And then, when she saw him looking crestfallen, she hurried on: 'But they are very pretty, and you did remember... Actually, they're just as nice as red and gold bangles! Come into the house when you are ready. I have made something special for you.'

'I am coming,' said Bisnu, turning towards the house. 'You don't know how hungry a man gets, walking five miles to reach home!'

BE PREPARED

I was a Boy Scout once, although I couldn't tell a slip knot from a granny knot, nor a reef knot from a thief knot. I did know that a thief knot was to be used to tie up a thief, should you happen to catch one. I have never caught a thief—and wouldn't know what to do with one since I can't tie the right knot. I'd just let him go with a warning, I suppose. And tell him to become a Boy Scout.

'Be prepared!' That's the Boy Scout motto. And it is a good one, too. But I never seem to be well prepared for anything, be it an exam or a journey or the roof blowing off my room. I get halfway through a speech and then forget what I have to say next. Or I make a new suit to attend a friend's wedding, and then turn up in my pyjamas.

So, how did I, the most impractical of boys, survive as a Boy Scout?

Well, it seems a rumour had gone around the junior school (I was still a junior then) that I was a good cook. I had never cooked anything in my life, but of course I had spent a lot of time in the tuck shop making suggestions and advising Chimpu, who ran the tuck shop, and encouraging him to make more and better samosas, jalebies, tikkees and pakoras. For my unwanted advice, he would favour me with an occasional free samosa. So, naturally, I looked upon him as a friend and benefactor. With this qualification, I was given a cookery badge and put in charge of our troop's supply of rations.

There were about twenty of us in our troop. During the summer break our Scoutmaster, Mr Oliver, took us on a camping expedition to Taradevi, a temple-crowned mountain a few miles outside Shimla. That first night we were put to work, peeling potatoes, skinning onions, shelling peas and pounding masalas. These various ingredients being ready, I was asked, as the troop cookery expert, what should be done with them.

'Put everything in that big degchi,' I ordered. 'Pour half a tin of ghee over the lot. Add some nettle leaves and cook for half an hour.'

When this was done, everyone had a taste, but the general opinion was that the dish lacked something.

'More salt,' I suggested.

More salt was added. It still lacked something.

'Add a cup of sugar,' I ordered.

Sugar was added to the concoction, but it still lacked something.

'We forgot to add tomatoes,' said one of the Scouts.

'Never mind,' I said. 'We have tomato sauce. Add a bottle of tomato sauce!'

'How about some vinegar?' suggested another boy.

'Just the thing,' I said. 'Add a cup of vinegar!'

'Now it's too sour,' said one of the tasters.

'What jam did we bring?' I asked.

'Gooseberry jam.'

'Just the thing. Empty the bottle!'

The dish was a great success. Everyone enjoyed it, including

Mr Oliver, who had no idea what had gone into it.

'What's this called?' he asked.

'It's an all-Indian sweet-and-sour jam-potato curry,' I ventured.

'For short, just call it *Bond bhujjia*,' said one of the boys.

I had earned my cookery badge!

Poor Mr Oliver; he wasn't really cut out to be a Scoutmaster, any more than I was meant to be a Scout.

The following day, he told us he would give us a lesson in tracking. Taking a half-hour start, he walked into the forest, leaving behind him a trail of broken twigs, chicken feathers, pine cones and chestnuts. We were to follow the trail until we found him.

Unfortunately, we were not very good trackers. We did follow Mr Oliver's trail some way into the forest, but then we were distracted by a pool of clear water. It looked very inviting. Abandoning our uniforms, we jumped into the pool and had a great time romping about or just lying on its grassy banks and enjoying the sunshine. Many hours later, feeling hungry, we returned to our campsite and set about preparing the evening meal. It was Bond bhujjia again, but with a few variations.

It was growing dark, and we were beginning to worry about Mr Oliver's whereabouts when he limped into the camp, assisted by a couple of local villagers. Having waited for us at the far end of the forest for a couple of hours, he had decided to return by following his own trail, but in the gathering gloom he was soon lost. Village folk returning home from the temple took charge and escorted him back to the camp. He was very angry and made us return all our good-conduct and other badges, which he stuffed into his haversack. I had to give up my cookery badge.

An hour later, when we were all preparing to get into

our sleeping bags for the night, Mr Oliver called out, 'Where's dinner?'

'We've had ours,' said one of the boys. 'Everything is finished, sir.'

'Where's Bond? He's supposed to be the cook. Bond, get up and make me an omelette.'

'I can't, sir.'

'Why not?'

'You have my badge. Not allowed to cook without it. Scout rule, sir.'

'I've never heard of such a rule. But you can take your badges, all of you. We return to school tomorrow.'

Mr Oliver returned to his tent in a huff.

But I relented and made him a grand omelette, garnishing it with dandelion leaves and a chilli.

'Never had such an omelette before,' confessed Mr Oliver.

'Would you like another, sir?'

'Tomorrow, Bond, tomorrow. We'll breakfast early tomorrow.'

But we had to break up our camp before we could do that because in the early hours of the next morning, a bear strayed into our camp, entered the tent where our stores were kept, and created havoc with all our provisions, even rolling our biggest degchi down the hillside.

In the confusion and uproar that followed, the bear entered Mr Oliver's tent (our Scoutmaster was already outside, fortunately) and came out entangled in his dressing gown. It then made off towards the forest, a comical sight in its borrowed clothes.

And though we were a troop of brave little scouts, we thought it better to let the bear keep the gown.

MISS BABCOCK'S BIG TOE

If two people are thrown together for a long time, they can became either close friends or sworn enemies. Thus, it was with Tata and me when we both went down with mumps and had to spend a fortnight together in the school hospital. It wasn't really a hospital—just a five-bed ward in a small cottage on the approach road to our prep-school in Chhota Shimla. It was supervised by a retired nurse, an elderly matron called Miss Babcock, who was all but stone deaf.

Miss Babcock was an able nurse, but she was a fidgety, fussy person, always dashing about from ward to dispensary and to her own room, as a result the boys called her Miss Shuttlecock. As she couldn't hear us, she didn't mind. But her hearing difficulty did create something of a problem, both for her and for her patients. If someone in the ward felt ill late at night, he had to shout or ring a bell, and she heard neither. So, someone had to get up and fetch her.

Miss Babcock devised an ingenious method of waking her in an emergency. She tied a long piece of string to the foot of the sick person's bed; then took the other end of the string to her own room, where, upon retiring for the night, she tied it to her big toe.

A vigorous pull on the string from the sick person, and Miss Babcock would be wide awake!

Now, what could be more tempting to a small boy than— such a device? The string was tied to the foot of Tata's bed, and he was a restless fellow, always wanting water, always complaining of aches and pains. And sometimes, out of plain mischief, he would give several tugs on that string until Miss Babcock arrived with a pill or a glass of water.

'You'll have my toe off by morning,' she complained. 'You don't have to pull quite so hard.'

And what was worse, when Tata did fall asleep, he snored to high heaven and nothing could wake him! I had to lie awake most of the night, listening to his rhythmic snoring. It was like a trumpet tuning up or a bullfrog calling to its mates.

Fortunately, a couple of nights later, we were joined in the ward by Bimal, a friend and fellow 'feather', who had also contracted mumps. One night of Tata's snoring, and Bimal resolved to do something about it.

'Wait until he's fast asleep,' said Bimal, 'and then we'll carry his bed outside and leave him in the veranda.' We did more than that. As Tata commenced his nightly imitation of all the wind instruments in the London Philharmonic Orchestra, we lifted up his bed as gently as possible and carried it out into the garden, putting it down beneath the nearest pine tree.

'It's healthier outside,' said Bimal, justifying our action. 'All this fresh air should cure him.'

Leaving Tata to serenade the stars, we returned to the ward expecting to enjoy a good night's sleep. So did Miss Babcock.

However, we couldn't sleep long. We were woken by Miss Babcock running around the ward screaming, 'Where's Tata? Where's Tata?' She ran outside, and we followed dutifully, barefoot, in our pyjamas.

The bed stood where we had put it down, but of Tata, there was no sign. Instead, there was a large black-faced langur at the foot of the bed, baring its teeth in a grin of disfavour.

'Tata's gone,' gasped Miss Babcock.

'He must be a sleepwalker,' said Bimal.

'Maybe the leopard took him,' I said. Just then there was a commotion in the shrubbery at the end of the garden and shouting, 'Help, help!' Tata emerged from the bushes, followed by several lithe, long-tailed langurs, merrily giving chase. Apparently, he'd woken up at the crack of dawn to find his bed surrounded by a gang of inquisitive simians. They had meant no harm, but Tata had panicked, and made a dash for life and liberty, running into the forest instead of into the cottage. We got Tata and his bed back into the ward, and Miss Babcock took his temperature and gave him a dose of salts. Oddly enough, in all the excitement no one asked how Tata and his bed had travelled in the night.

And strangely, he did not snore the following night; so perhaps the pine-scented night air really helped. Needless to say, we all soon recovered from the mumps, and Miss Babcock's big toe received a well-deserved rest.

UNCLE KEN'S RUMBLE
IN THE JUNGLE

Uncle Ken drove Grandfather's old Fiat along the Forest Road at an incredible 30mph, scattering pheasants, partridges and junglefowl as he scattered along. He had come in search of the disappearing red junglefowl, and I could see why the bird had disappeared. Too many noisy human beings had invaded its habitat.

By the time we reached the forest rest house, one of the car doors had fallen off its hinges, and a large lantana bush had got entwined in the bumper.

'Never mind,' said Uncle Ken. 'It's all part of the adventure.'

The rest house had been reserved for Uncle Ken, thanks to Grandfather's good relations with the forest department. But I was the only other person in the car. No one else would trust himself or herself to Uncle Ken's driving. He treated a car as though it were a low-flying aircraft having some difficulty in getting off the runway.

As we arrived at the rest house, a number of hens made a dash for safety.

'Look, junglefowl!' exclaimed Uncle Ken.

'Domestic fowl,' I said, 'They must belong to the forest guards.'

I was right, of course. One of the hens was destined to be served up as chicken curry later that day. The jungle birds avoided the neighbourhood of the rest house, just in case they were mistaken for poultry and went into the cooking-pot.

Uncle Ken was all for starting his search right away, and after a brief interval during which we were served with tea and pakoras (prepared by the forest guard, who it turned out was also a good cook), we set off on foot into the jungle in search of the elusive red junglefowl.

'No tigers around here! Are there?' asked Uncle Ken, just to be on the safe side.

'No tigers on this range,' said the guard, 'Just elephants.'

Uncle Ken wasn't afraid of elephants. He'd been for numerous elephants rides at the Lucknow zoo. He'd also seen Sabu in *Elephant Boy*.

A small wooden bridge took us across a little river, and then we were in thick jungle, following the forest guard who led us along a path that was frequently blocked by broken tree branches and pieces of bamboo.

'Why all these broken branches?' asked Uncle Ken.

'The elephants, sir,' replied our guard, 'They passed through last night. They like certain leaves, as well as young bamboo shoots.'

We saw a number of spotted deer and several pheasants, but no red junglefowl.

That evening we sat out on the verandah of the rest house. All was silent except for the distant trumpeting of elephants. Then, from the stream, came the chanting of hundreds of frogs.

There were tenors and baritones, sopranos and contraltos

and occasionally a bass deep enough to have pleased the great Chaliapin. They sang duets and quartets from *La Boheme* and other Italian operas, drowning out all other jungle sounds except for the occasional cry of a jackal doing his best to join in.

'We might as well sing too,' said Uncle Ken, and began singing the 'Indian Love Call' in his best Nelson Eddy manner.

The frogs fell silent, obviously awestruck; but instead of receiving an answering love-call, Uncle Ken was answered by even more strident jackal calls—not one, but several—with the result that all self-respecting denizens of the forest fled from the vicinity, and we saw no wildlife that night apart from a frightened rabbit that sped across the clearing and vanished into the darkness.

Early next morning we renewed our efforts to track down the Red junglefowl, but it remained elusive. Returning to the rest house dusty and weary, Uncle Ken exclaimed: 'There it is—a Red junglefowl!'

But it turned out to be the caretaker's cock-bird, a handsome fellow all red and gold, but not the jungle variety.

Disappointed, Uncle Ken decided to return to civilization. Another night in the rest house did not appeal to him. He had run out of songs to sing.

In any case, the weather had changed overnight and a light drizzle was falling as we started out. This had turned to a steady downpour by the time we reached the bridge across the Suseva River. And standing in the middle of the bridge was an elephant.

He was a long tusker and he didn't look too friendly.

Uncle Ken blew his horn, and that was a mistake.

It was a strident, penetrating horn, highly effective on city roads but out of place in the forest.

The elephant took it as a challenge, and returned the blast

of the horn with a shrill trumpeting of its own. It took a few steps forward. Uncle Ken put the car into reverse.

'Is there another way out of here?' he asked.

'There's a side road,' I said, recalling an earlier trip with Grandfather, 'It will take us to the Kansrao railway station.'

'What ho!' cried Uncle Ken. 'To the station we go!'

And he turned the car and drove back until we came to the turning.

The narrow road was now a rushing torrent of rain water and all Uncle Ken's driving-skills were put to the test. He had on one occasion driven through a brick wall, so he knew all about obstacles; but they were usually stationary ones.

'More elephants,' I said, as two large pachyderms loomed out of the rain-drenched forest.

'Elephants to the right of us, elephants to the left of us!' chanted Uncle Ken, misquoting Tennyson's 'The Charge of the Light Brigade', 'Into the valley of death rode the six hundred!'

'There are now three of them,' I observed.

'Not my lucky number,' said Uncle Ken and pressed hard on the accelerator. We lurched forward, almost running over a terrified barking-deer.

'Is four your lucky number, Uncle Ken?'

'Why do you ask?'

'Well, there are now four of them behind us. And they are catching up quite fast!'

'I see the station ahead,' cried Uncle Ken, as we drove into a clearing where a tiny railway station stood like a beacon of safety in the wilderness.

The car came to a grinding halt. We abandoned it and ran for the building.

The station-master saw our predicament, and beckoned to

us to enter the station building, which was little more than a two-room shed and platform. He took us inside his tiny control room and shut the steel gate behind us.

'The elephants won't bother you here,' he said. 'But say goodbye to your car.'

We looked out of the window and were horrified to see Grandfather's Fiat overturned by one of the elephants, while another proceeded to trample it underfoot. The other elephants joined in the mayhem and soon the car was a flattened piece of junk.

'I'm station-master Abdul Rauf,' the station-master introduced himself. 'I know a good scrap dealer in Doiwala. I'll give you his address.'

'But how do we get out of here?' asked Uncle Ken.

'Well, it's only an hour's walk to Doiwala, not with those elephants around. Stay and have a cup of tea. The Dehra Express will pass through shortly. It stops for a few minutes. And it's only half-an-hour to Dehra from here.' He punched out a couple of rail tickets, 'Here you are, my friends. Just two rupees each. The cheapest rail journey in India. And these tickets carry an insurance value of two lakh rupees each, should an accident befall you between here and Dehradun.'

Uncle Ken's eyes lit up.

'You mean, if one of us falls out of the train?' he asked.

'Out of the moving train,' clarified the station-master. 'There will be an enquiry, of course, some people try to fake an accident.'

But Uncle Ken decided against falling out of the train and making a fortune. He'd had enough excitement for the day. We got home safely enough, taking a pony-cart from Dehradun station to our house.

'Where's my car?' asked Grandfather, as we staggered up the verandah steps.

'It had a small accident,' said Uncle Ken. 'We left it outside the Kansrao railway station. I'll collect it later.'

'I'm starving,' I said. 'Haven't eaten since morning.'

'Well, come and have your dinner,' said Granny. 'I've made something special for you. One of your grandfather's hunting friends sent us a junglefowl. I've made a nice roast. Try it with apple sauce.'

Uncle Ken did not ask if the junglefowl was red, grey, or techni-coloured. He was first to the dining table.

Granny had anticipated this, and served me with a chicken leg, giving the other leg to grandfather.

'I rather fancy the breast myself,' she said, and this left Uncle Ken with a long and scrawny neck—which was more than he deserved.

THE PLAYING FIELDS OF SIMLA

It had been a lonely winter for a twelve-year-old boy. I hadn't really got over my father's untimely death two years ago; nor had I as yet reconciled myself to my mother's marriage to the Punjabi gentleman who dealt in second-hand cars. The three-month winter break over, I was almost happy to return to my boarding school in Simla—that elegant hill station once celebrated by Kipling and soon to lose its status as the summer capital of the Raj in India.

It wasn't as though I had many friends at school. I had always been a bit of a loner, shy and reserved, looking out only for my father's rare visits—on his brief leaves from RAF duties—and to my sharing his tent or air-force hutment outside Delhi or Karachi. Those unsettled but happy days would not come again. I needed a friend but it was not easy to find one among a horde of rowdy, pea-shooting fourth formers, who carved their names on desks and stuck chewing gum on the class teacher's chair. Had I grown up with other children, I might have developed a taste for schoolboy anarchy; but, in sharing my father's loneliness after his separation from my mother, I had turned into a premature adult. The mixed nature of my reading—Dickens, Richmal Crompton, Tagore and *Champion* and

Film Fun comics—probably reflected the confused state of my life. A book reader was rare even in those pre-electronic times. On rainy days most boys played cards or Monopoly, or listened to Artie Shaw on the wind-up gramophone in the common room.

After a month in the fourth form I began to notice a new boy, Omar, and then only because he was a quiet, almost taciturn person who took no part in the form's feverish attempts to imitate the Marx Brothers at the circus. He showed no resentment at the prevailing anarchy, nor did he make a move to participate in it. Once he caught me looking at him, and he smiled ruefully, tolerantly. Did I sense another adult in the class? Someone who was a little older than his years?

Even before we began talking to each other, Omar and I developed an understanding of sorts, and we'd nod almost respectfully to each other when we met in the classroom corridors or the environs of dining hall or dormitory. We were not in the same house. The house system practised its own form of apartheid, whereby a member of, say, Curzon House was not expected to fraternize with someone belonging to Rivaz or Lefroy! Those public schools certainly knew how to clamp you into compartments. However, these barriers vanished when Omar and I found ourselves selected for the School Colts' hockey team—Omar as a fullback, I as goalkeeper. I think a defensive position suited me by nature. In all modesty I have to say that I made a good goalkeeper, both at hockey and football. And fifty years on, I am still keeping goal. Then I did it between goalposts, now I do it off the field—protecting a family, protecting my independence as a writer...

The taciturn Omar now spoke to me occasionally, and we combined well on the field of play. A good understanding is needed between goalkeeper and fullback. We were on the same wavelength. I anticipated his moves, he was familiar with mine. Years later, when I read Conrad's *The Secret Sharer*, I thought of Omar.

It wasn't until we were away from the confines of school, classroom and dining hall, that our friendship flourished. The hockey team travelled to Sanawar on the next mountain range, where we were to play a couple of matches against our old rivals, the Lawrence Royal Military School. This had been my father's old school, but I did not know that in his time it had also been a military orphanage. Grandfather, who had been a private foot soldier—of the likes of Kipling's Mulvaney, Otheris and Learoyd—had joined the Scottish Rifles after leaving home at the age of seventeen. He had died while his children were still very young, but my father's more rounded education had enabled him to become an officer.

Omar and I were thrown together a good deal during the visit to Sanawar, and in our more leisurely moments, strolling undisturbed around a school where we were guests and not pupils, we exchanged life histories and other confidences. Omar, too, had lost his father—had I sensed that before?—shot in some tribal encounter on the Frontier, for he hailed from the lawless lands beyond Peshawar. A wealthy uncle was seeing to Omar's education. The RAF was now seeing to mine.

We wandered into the school chapel, and there I found my father's name—A.A. Bond—on the school's roll of honour board: old boys who had lost their lives while serving during the two World Wars.

'What did his initials stand for?' asked Omar.

'Aubrey Alexander.'

'Unusual names, like yours. Why did your parents call you Ruskin?'

'I am not sure. I think my father liked the works of John Ruskin, who wrote on serious subjects like art and architecture. I don't think anyone reads him now. They'll read me, though!' I had already started writing my first book. It was called *Nine Months* (the length of the school term, not a pregnancy), and it described some of the happenings at school and lampooned a few of our teachers. I had filled three slim exercise books with this premature literary project, and I allowed Omar to go through them. He must have been my first reader and critic. 'They're very interesting,' he said, 'but you'll get into trouble if someone finds them. Especially Mr Oliver.' And he read out an offending verse:

> Olly, Olly, Olly, with his balls on a trolley,
> And his arse all painted green!

I have to admit it wasn't great literature. I was better at hockey and football. I made some spectacular saves, and we won our matches against Sanawar. When we returned to Simla, we were school heroes for a couple of days and lost some of our reticence; we were even a little more forthcoming with other boys. And then Mr Fisher, my housemaster, discovered my literary opus, *Nine Months,* under my mattress, and took it away and read it (as he told me later) from cover to cover. Corporal punishment then being in vogue, I was given six of the best with a springy malacca cane, and my manuscript was torn up and deposited in Fisher's wastepaper basket. All I had to show for my efforts were some purple welts on my bottom. These were proudly displayed to all who were interested, and I was a hero for another two days.

'Will you go away too when the British leave India?' Omar asked me one day.

'I don't think so,' I said. 'My stepfather is Indian.'

'Everyone is saying that our leaders and the British are going to divide the country. Simla will be in India, Peshawar in Pakistan!'

'Oh, it won't happen,' I said glibly. 'How can they cut up such a big country?' But even as we chatted about the possibility, Nehru and Jinnah and Mountbatten and all those who mattered were preparing their instruments for major surgery.

Before their decision impinged on our lives and everyone else's, we found a little freedom of our own—in an underground tunnel that we discovered below the third flat.

It was really part of an old, disused drainage system, and when Omar and I began exploring it, we had no idea just how far it extended. After crawling along on our bellies for some twenty feet, we found ourselves in complete darkness. Omar had brought along a small pencil torch, and with its help we continued writhing forward (moving backwards would have been quite impossible) until we saw a glimmer of light at the end of the tunnel. Dusty, musty, very scruffy, we emerged at last onto a grassy knoll, a little way outside the school boundary.

It's always a great thrill to escape beyond the boundaries that adults have devised. Here we were in unknown territory. To travel without passports—that would be the ultimate freedom!

But more passports were on their way and more boundaries.

Lord Mountbatten, viceroy and governor-general-to-be, came for our Founder's Day and gave away the prizes. I had won a prize for something or the other, and mounted the rostrum to receive my book from this towering, handsome man in his pinstriped suit. Bishop Cotton's was then the premier school of India, often referred to as the 'Eton of the East'. Viceroys and governors had graced its functions. Many of its boys had gone on to eminence in the civil services and armed forces. There was one 'old boy' about whom they maintained a stolid silence—General Dyer, who had ordered the massacre at Amritsar and destroyed the trust that had been building up between Britain and India.

Now Mountbatten spoke of the momentous events that were happening all around us—the War had just come to an end, the United Nations held out the promise of a world living in peace and harmony, and India, an equal partner with Britain, would be among the great nations...

A few weeks later, Bengal and Punjab provinces were bisected. Riots flared up across northern India, and there was a great exodus of people crossing the newly drawn frontiers of Pakistan and India. Homes were destroyed, thousands lost their lives.

The common-room radio and the occasional newspaper kept us abreast of events, but in our tunnel, Omar and I felt immune from all that was happening, worlds away from all the pillage, murder and revenge. And outside the tunnel, on the pine knoll below the school, there was fresh untrodden grass, sprinkled with clover and daisies, the only sounds the hammering of a woodpecker, the distant insistent call of the Himalayan barbet. Who could touch us there?

'And when all the wars are done,' I said, 'a butterfly will still be beautiful.'

'Did you read that somewhere?'

'No, it just came into my head.'

'Already you're a writer.'

'No, I want to play hockey for India or football for Arsenal. Only winning teams!'

'You can't win forever. Better to be a writer.'

When the monsoon rains arrived, the tunnel was flooded, the drain choked with rubble. We were allowed out to the cinema to see Lawrence Olivier's *Hamlet*, a film that did nothing to raise our spirits on a wet and gloomy afternoon—but it was our last picture that year, because communal riots suddenly broke out in Simla's Lower Bazaar, an area that was still much as Kipling had described it—'a man who knows his way there can defy all the police of India's summer capital'—and we were confined to school indefinitely.

One morning after chapel, the headmaster announced that the Muslim boys—those who had their homes in what was now Pakistan—would have to be evacuated, sent to their homes across the border with an armed convoy.

The tunnel no longer provided an escape for us. The bazaar was out of bounds. The flooded playing field was deserted. Omar and I sat on a damp wooden bench and talked about the future in vaguely hopeful terms; but we didn't solve any problems. Mountbatten and Nehru and Jinnah were doing all the solving.

It was soon time for Omar to leave—he along with some fifty other boys from Lahore, Pindi and Peshawar. The rest of us—Hindus, Christians, Parsis—helped them load their luggage into the waiting trucks. A couple of boys broke down and wept. So did our departing school captain, a Pathan who had been known for his stoic and unemotional demeanour. Omar waved cheerfully to me and I waved back. We had vowed to meet again some day.

The convoy got through safely enough. There was only one casualty—the school cook, who had strayed into an off-limits area in the foothill town of Kalka and been set upon by a mob. He wasn't seen again.

Towards the end of the school year, just as we were all

getting ready to leave for the school holidays, I received a letter from Omar. He told me something about his new school and how he missed my company and our games and our tunnel to freedom. I replied and gave him my home address, but I did not hear from him again. The land, though divided, was still a big one, and we were very small.

Some seventeen or eighteen years later I did get news of Omar, but in an entirely different context. India and Pakistan were at war and in a bombing raid over Ambala, not far from Simla, a Pakistani plane was shot down. Its crew died in the crash. One of them, I learnt later, was Omar.

Did he, I wonder, get a glimpse of the playing fields we knew so well as boys?

Perhaps memories of his schooldays flooded back as he flew over the foothills. Perhaps he remembered the tunnel through which we were able to make our little escape to freedom.

But there are no tunnels in the sky.

THE CANAL

We loved to bathe there, on hot summer afternoons—Sushil and Raju and Pitamber and I—and there were others as well, but we were the regulars, the ones who met at other times too, eating at chaat-shops or riding on bicycles into the tea-gardens.

The canal has disappeared—or rather, it has gone underground, having been covered over with concrete to widen the road to which it ran parallel for most of its way. Here and there it went through a couple of large properties, and it was at the extremity of one of these—just inside the boundaries of Miss Gamla's house—that the canal went into a loop, where it was joined by another small canal, and this was the best place for bathing or just romping around. The smaller boys wore nothing, but we had just reached the years of puberty and kept our kachhas on. So Miss Gamla really had nothing to complain about.

I'm not sure if this was her real name. I think we called her Miss Gamla because of the large number of gamlas or flowerpots that surrounded her house. They filled the verandah, decorated the windows, and lined the approach road. She had a mali who was always watering the pots. And there was no shortage of water, the canal being nearby.

But Miss Gamla did not like small boys. Or big boys, for that matter. She placed us high on her list of pests, along with monkeys (who raided her kitchen), sparrows (who shattered her sweet-peas), and goats (who ate her geraniums). We did none of these things, being strictly fun-loving creatures; but we did make a lot of noise, spoiling her afternoon siesta. And I think she was offended by the sight of our near-naked bodies cavorting about on the boundaries of her estate. A spinster in her sixties, the proximity of naked flesh, no matter how immature, disturbed and upset her.

She had a companion—a noisy peke, who followed her around everywhere and set up an ear-splitting barking at anyone who came near. It was the barking, rather than our play, that woke her in the afternoons. And then she would emerge from her back verandah, waving a stick at us, and shouting at us to be off.

We would collect our clothes, and lurk behind a screen of lantana bushes, returning to the canal as soon as lady and dog were back in the house.

The canal came down from the foothills, from a hill called Nalapani where a famous battle had taken place a hundred and fifty years back, between the British and the Gurkhas. But for some quirky reason, possibly because we were not very good at history, we called it the Panipat canal, after a more famous battle north of Delhi.

We had our own mock battles, wrestling on the grassy banks of the canal before plunging into the water—it was no more man waist-high—flailing around with shouts of joy, with no one to hinder our animal spirits...

Except Miss Gamla.

Down the path she hobbled—she had a pronounced limp—waving her walnut-wood walking-stick at us, while her bulging-eyed peke came yapping at her heels.

'Be off, you chhokra-boys!' she'd shout. 'Off to your filthy homes, or I'll put the police on to you!'

And on one occasion she did report us to the local thana, and a couple of policemen came along, told us to get dressed and warned us off the property. But the Head Constable was Pitamber's brother-in-law's brother-in-law, so the ban did not last for more than a couple of days. We were soon back at our favourite stretch of canal.

When Miss Gamla saw that we were back, as merry and disrespectful as ever, she was furious. She nearly had a fit when Raju—probably the most wicked of the four of us—did a jig in front of her, completely in the nude.

When Miss Gamla advanced upon him, stick raised, he jumped into the canal.

'Why don't you join us?' shouted Sushil, taunting the enraged woman.

'Jump in and cool off,' I called, not to be outdone in villainy.

The little peke ran up and down the banks of the canal, yapping furiously, dying to sink its teeth into our bottoms. Miss Gamla came right down to the edge of the canal, waving her stick, trying to connect with any part of Raju's anatomy that could be reached. The ferrule of the stick caught him on the shoulder and he gave a yelp of pain. Miss Gamla gave a shrill cry of delight. She had scored a hit!

She made another lunge at Raju, and this time I caught the end of the stick and pulled. Instead of letting go of the stick, Miss Gamla hung on to it. I should have let go then, but on an impulse I gave it a short, sharp pull, and to my horror, both walking-stick and Miss Gamla tumbled into the canal.

Miss Gamla went under for a few seconds. Then she came to the surface, spluttering, and screamed. There was a frenzy of barking from the peke. Why had he been left out of the game? Wisely, he forbore from joining us.

We went to the aid of Miss Gamla, with every intention of pulling her out of the canal, but she backed away, screaming, 'Get away from me, get away!' Fortunately, the walking-stick had been carried away by the current.

Miss Gamla was now in danger of being carried away too. Floundering about, she had backed away to a point where a secondary canal joined the first, and here the current was swift. Even the boys, big and small, avoided that spot. It formed a little whirlpool before rushing on.

'Memsahib, be careful!' shouted Pitamber.

'Watch out!' I shouted. 'You won't be able to stand against the current.'

Raju and Sushil lunged forward to help, but with a look of hatred Miss Gamla turned away and tried to walk downstream. A surge in the current swept her off her legs. Her gown billowed up, turning her into a sail-boat, and she moved slowly downstream, arms flailing as she tried to regain her balance.

We scrambled out of the canal and ran along the bank, hoping to overtake her, but we were hindered by the peke who kept snapping at our heels, and by the fact that we were without our clothes and approaching the busy Dilaram Bazaar.

Just before the Bazaar, the canal went underground, emerging about two hundred metres further on, at the junction of the Old Survey Road and the East Canal Road. To our horror, we saw Miss Gamla float into the narrow tunnel that carried the canal along its underground journey. If she didn't get stuck somewhere in the channel, she would emerge—hopefully, still alive—at the other end of the passage.

We ran back for our clothes, dressed, then ran through the Bazaar, and did not stop running until we reached the exit point on the Canal Road. This must have taken us ten to fifteen minutes.

We took up our positions on the culvert where the canal emerged, and waited.

We waited and waited.

No sign of Miss Gamla.

'She must be stuck somewhere,' said Pitamber.

'She'll drown,' said Sushil.

'Not our fault,' said Raju. 'If we tell anyone, we'll get into trouble. They'll think we pushed her in.'

'We'll wait a little longer,' I said.

So we hung about the canal banks, pretending to catch tadpoles, and hoping that Miss Gamla would emerge—preferably alive.

Her walking-stick floated past. We did not touch it. It would be evidence against us, said Pitamber. The dog had gone home after seeing his mistress disappear down the tunnel.

'Like Alice,' I thought. 'Only that was a dream.'

When it grew dark, we went our different ways, resolving not to mention the episode to anyone. We might be accused of murder! By now, we felt like murderers.

A week passed, and nothing happened. No bloated body was found floating in the lower reaches of the canal. No Memsahib was reported missing.

They say the guilty always return to the scene of the crime. More out of curiosity than guilt, we came together one afternoon, just before the rains broke, and crept through the shrubbery behind Miss Gamla's house.

All was silent, all was still. No one was playing in the canal. The mango trees were unattended. No one touched Miss Gamla's mangoes. Trespassers were more afraid of her than of her lathi-wielding mali.

We crept out of the bushes and advanced towards the cool, welcoming water flowing past us.

And then came a shout from the house.

'Scoundrels! Goondas! Chhokra-boys! I'll catch you diis time!'

And there stood Miss Gamla, tall and menacing, alive and well, flourishing a brand new walking-stick and advancing down her steps.

'It's her ghost!' gasped Raju.

'No, she's real,' said Sushil. 'Must have got out of the canal somehow.'

'Well, at least we aren't murderers,' said Pitamber.

'No,' I said. 'But she'll murder us if we stand here any longer.'

Miss Gamla had been joined by her mali, the yelping peke, and a couple of other retainers.

'Let's go,' said Raju.

We fled the scene. And we never went there again. Miss Gamla had won the Battle of Panipat.

TIGERS FOREVER

On the left bank of the river Ganges, where it flows out from the Himalayan foothills, is a long stretch of heavy forest. There are villages on the fringe of the forest, inhabited by farmers and herdsmen. Big-game hunters came to the area for many years, and as a result the animals had been getting fewer. The trees, too, had been disappearing slowly; and as the animals lost their food and shelter, they moved further into the foothills.

There was a time when this forest had provided a home for some thirty to forty tigers, but men in search of skins and trophies had shot them all, and now there remained only one old tiger in the jungle. The hunters had tried to get him, too, but he was a wise and crafty tiger, who knew the ways of man, and so far he had survived all attempts on his life.

Although the tiger had passed the prime of his life, he had lost none of his majesty. His muscles rippled beneath the golden yellow of his coat, and he walked through the long grass with the confidence of one who knew that he was still a king, although his subjects were fewer. His great head pushed through the foliage, and it was only his tail, swinging high, that sometimes showed above the sea of grass.

He was heading for water, the water of a large marsh, where he sometimes went to drink or cool off. The marsh was usually deserted except when the buffaloes from a nearby village were brought there to bathe or wallow in the muddy water.

The tiger waited in the shelter of a rock, his ears pricked for any unfamiliar sound. He knew that it was here that hunters sometimes waited for him with guns.

He walked into the water, amongst the water-lilies, and drank slowly. He was seldom in a hurry when he ate or drank.

He raised his head and listened, one paw suspended in the air.

A strange sound had come to him on the breeze, and he was wary of strange sounds. So he moved swiftly into the shelter of the tall grass that bordered the marsh, and climbed a hillock until he reached his favourite rock. This rock was big enough to hide him and to give him shade.

The sound he had heard was only a flute, sounding thin and reedy in the forest. It belonged to Nandu, a slim brown boy who rode a buffalo. Nandu played vigorously on the flute. Chottu, a slightly smaller boy, riding another buffalo, brought up the rear of the herd.

There were eight buffaloes in the herd, which belonged to the families of Nandu and Chottu, who were cousins. Their fathers sold buffalo-milk and butter in villages further down the river.

The tiger had often seen them at the marsh, and he was not bothered by their presence. He knew the village folk would leave him alone as long as he did not attack their buffaloes. And as long as there were deer in the jungle, he would not be interested in other prey.

He decided to move on and find a cool shady place in the heart of the jungle, where he could rest during the hot afternoon and be free of the flies and mosquitoes that swarmed around the marsh. At night he would hunt.

With a lazy grunt that was half a roar, 'A-oonh!'—he got off his haunches and sauntered off into the jungle.

The gentlest of tigers' roars can be heard a mile away, and the boys, who were barely fifty yards distant, looked up immediately.

'There he goes!' said Nandu, taking the flute from his lips and pointing with it towards the hillock. 'Did you see him?'

'I saw his tail, just before he disappeared. He's a big tiger!'

'Don't call him tiger. Call him Uncle.'

'Why?' asked Chottu.

'Because it's unlucky to call a tiger a tiger. My father told me so. But if you meet a tiger, and call him Uncle, he will leave you alone.'

'I see,' said Chottu. 'You have to make him a relative. I'll try and remember that.'

The buffaloes were now well into the march, and some of them were lying down in the mud. Buffaloes love soft wet mud and will wallow in it for hours. Nandu and Chottu were not so fond of the mud, so they went swimming in deeper water. Later, they rested in the shade of an old silk-cotton tree.

It was evening, and the twilight fading fast, when the buffalo herd finally made its way homeward, to be greeted outside the village by the barking of dogs, the gurgle of hookah-pipes, and the homely smell of cow-dung smoke.

2

The following evening, when Nandu and Chottu came home with the buffalo herd, they found a crowd of curious villagers surrounding a jeep in which sat three strangers with guns. They were hunters, and they were accompanied by servants and a large store of provisions.

They had heard that there was a tiger in the area, and they wanted to shoot it.

These men had money to spend; and, as most of the villagers were poor, they were prepared to go into the forest to make a machaan or tree-platform for the hunters. The platform, big enough to take the three men, was put up in the branches of a tall mahogany tree.

Nandu was told by his father to tie a goat at the foot of the tree. While these preparations were being made, Chottu slipped off and circled the area, with a plan of his own in mind. He had no wish to see the tiger killed and he had decided to give it some sort of warning. So he tied up bits and pieces of old clothing on small trees and bushes. He knew the wily old king of the jungle would keep well away from the area if he saw the bits of clothing—for where there were men's clothes, there would be men.

The vigil kept by the hunters lasted all through the night, but the tiger did not come near the tree. Perhaps he'd got Chottu's warning; or perhaps he wasn't hungry.

It was a cold night, and it wasn't long before the hunters opened their flasks of rum. Soon they were whispering among themselves; then they were chattering so loudly that no wild animal would have come anywhere near them. By morning they were fast asleep.

They looked grumpy and shamefaced as they trudged back to the village.

'Wrong time of the year for tiger,' said the first hunter.

'Nothing left in these parts,' said the second.

'I think I've caught a cold,' said the third. And they drove away in disgust.

It was not until the beginning of the summer that something happened to alter the hunting habits of the tiger and bring him into conflict with the villagers.

There had been no rain for almost two months, and the tall jungle grass had become a sea of billowy dry yellow. Some city-dwellers, camping near the forest, had been careless while cooking and had started a forest fire. Slowly it spread into the interior, from where the acrid fumes smoked the tiger out towards the edge of the jungle. As night came on, the flames grew more vivid, the smell stronger. The tiger turned and made for the marsh, where he knew he would be safe, provided he swam across to the little island in the centre.

Next morning he was on the island, which was untouched by the fire. But his surroundings had changed. The slopes of the hills were black with burnt grass, and most of the tall bamboo had disappeared. The deer and the wild pig, finding that their natural cover had gone, moved further east.

When the fire had died down and the smoke had cleared, the tiger prowled through the forest again but found no game. He drank at the marsh and settled down in a shady spot to sleep the day away.

The tiger spent four days looking for game. By that time he was so hungry that he even resorted to rooting among the dead leaves and burnt-out stumps of trees, searching for worms and beetles. This was a sad comedown for the king of the jungle.

But even now he hesitated to leave the area in search of new hunting grounds, for he had a deep fear and suspicion of the unknown forests further east—forests that were fast being swept away by human habitation. He could have gone north, into the high mountains, but they did not provide him with the long grass he needed for cover.

At break of day he came to the marsh. The water was now shallow and muddy, and a green scum had spread over the top. He drank, and then lay down across his favourite rock, hoping for a deer; but none came. He was about to get up and lope away when he heard an animal approach.

The tiger at once slipped off his rock and flattened himself on the ground, his tawny stripes merging with the dry grass.

A buffalo emerged from the jungle and came to the water. The buffalo was alone. He was a big male, and his long curved horns lay right back across his shoulders. He moved leisurely towards the water, completely unaware of the tiger's presence.

The tiger hesitated before making his charge.

It was a long time—many years—since he had killed a buffalo, and he knew instinctively that the villagers would be angry. But the pangs of hunger overcame his caution. There was no morning breeze, everything was still, and the smell of the tiger did not reach the buffalo. A monkey chattered on a nearby tree, but his warning went unheeded.

Crawling stealthily on his stomach, the tiger skirted the edge of the marsh and approached the buffalo from behind. The buffalo was standing in shallow water, drinking, when the tiger charged from the side and sank his teeth into his victim's thigh.

The buffalo staggered, but turned to fight. He snorted and lowered his horns at the tiger. But the big cat was too fast for the brave buffalo. He bit into the other leg and the buffalo crashed to the ground. Then the tiger moved in for the kill.

After resting, he began to eat. Although he had been starving for days, he could not finish the huge carcass. And so he quenched his thirst at the marsh and dragged the remains of the buffalo into the bushes, to conceal it from jackals and vultures; then he went off to find a place to sleep.

He would return to the kill when he was hungry.

3

The herdsmen were naturally very upset when they discovered that a buffalo was missing. And next day, when Nandu and Chottu came running home to say that they had found the half-eaten carcass near the marsh, the men of the village grew angry. They knew that once the tiger realised how easy it was to kill their animals, he would make a habit of doing so.

Kundan Singh, Nandu's father, who owned the buffalo, said he would go after the tiger himself.

'It's too late now,' said his wife. 'You should never have let the buffalo roam on its own.'

'He had been on his own before. This is the first time the tiger has attacked one of our animals.'

'He must have been hungry,' said Chottu.

'Well, we are hungry too,' said Kundan Singh. 'Our best buffalo—the only male in the herd. It will cost me at least two thousand rupees to buy another.'

'The tiger will kill again,' said Chottu's father. 'Many years ago there was a tiger who did the same thing. He became a cattle-killer.'

'Should we send for the hunters?'

'No, they are clumsy fools. The tiger will return to the

carcass for another meal. You have a gun?'

Kundan Singh smiled proudly and, going to a cupboard, brought out a double-barrelled gun. It looked ancient!

'My father bought it from an Englishman,' he said.

'How long ago was that?'

'About the time I was born.'

'And have you ever used it?' asked Chottu's father, looking at the old gun with distrust.

'A few years ago I let it off at some bandits. Don't you remember? When I fired, they did not stop running until they had crossed the river.'

'Yes, but did you hit anyone?'

'I would have, if someone's goat hadn't got in the way.'

'We had roast meat that night,' said Nandu.

Accompanied by Chottu's father and several others, Kundan set out for the marsh, where, without shifting the buffalo's carcass—for they knew the tiger would not come near them if he suspected a trap—they made another tree-platform in the branches of a tall tree some thirty feet from the kill.

Late that evening, Kundan Singh and Chottu's father settled down for the night on their rough platform.

Several hours passed and nothing but a jackal was seen by the watchers. And then, just as the moon came up over the distant hills, the two men were startled by a low 'A-oonh', followed by a suppressed, rumbling growl.

Kundan tightened his grip on the old gun. There was complete silence for a minute or two, then the sound of stealthy footfalls on the dead leaves beneath the tree.

A moment later, the tiger walked out into the moonlight and stood over his kill.

At first Kundan could do nothing. He was completely taken

aback by the size of the tiger. Chottu's father had to nudge him, and then Kundan quickly put the gun to his shoulder, aimed at the tiger's head, and pressed the trigger.

The gun went off with a flash and two loud bangs, as Kundan fired both barrels. There was a tremendous roar. The tiger rushed at the tree and tried to leap into the branches. Fortunately, the platform had been built at a good height, and the tiger was unable to reach it.

He roared again and then bounded off into the forest.

'What a tiger!' exclaimed Kundan, half in fear and half in admiration.

'You missed him completely,' said Chottu's father.

'I did not,' said Kundan. 'You heard him roar! Would he have been so angry if he had not been hit?'

'Well, if you have only wounded him, he will turn into a man-eater—and where will that leave us?'

'He won't be back,' said Kundan. 'He will leave this area.'

During the next few days the tiger lay low. He did not go near the marsh except when it was very dark and he was very thirsty. The herdsmen and villagers decided that the tiger had gone away. Nandu and Chottu—usually accompanied by other village youths, and always carrying their small hand-axes—began bringing the buffaloes to the marsh again during the day; they were careful not to let any of them stray far from the herd.

But one day, while the boys were taking the herd home, one of the buffaloes lagged behind. Nandu did not realise that an animal was missing until he heard an agonised bellow behind him. He glanced over his shoulder just in time to see the tiger dragging the buffalo into a clump of bamboo. The herd sensed the danger, and the buffaloes snorted with fear as they hurried along the forest path. To urge them forward and to warn his friends, Nandu cupped his hands to his mouth and gave a yodelling call.

The buffaloes bellowed, the boys shouted and the birds flew shrieking from the trees. Together they stampeded out of the forest. The villagers heard the thunder of hoofs, and saw the herd coming home amidst clouds of dust.

'The tiger!' called Nandu. 'He is back! He has taken another buffalo!'

'He is afraid of us no longer,' thought Chottu. And now everyone will hate him and do their best to kill him.

'Did you see where he went?' asked Kundan Singh, hurrying up to them.

'I remember the place,' said Nandu.

'Then there is no time to lose,' said Kundan. 'I will take my gun and a few men, and wait near the bridge. The rest of you must beat the jungle from this side and drive the tiger towards me. He will not escape this time, unless he swims across the river!'

4

Kundan took his men and headed for the suspension bridge over the river, while the others, guided by Nandu and Chottu, went to the spot where the tiger had seized the buffalo.

The tiger was still eating when he heard the men coming. He had not expected to be disturbed so soon. With an angry 'Whoof!' he bounded into the jungle, and watched the men—there were some twenty of them—through a screen of leaves and tall grass.

The men carried hand drums slung from their shoulders, and some carried sticks and spears. After a hurried consultation, they strung out in a line and entered the jungle beating their drums.

The tiger did not like the noise. He went deeper into the jungle. But the men came after him, banging away on their drums and shouting at the top of their voices. They advanced singly or in pairs, but nowhere were they more than fifteen yards apart.

The tiger could easily have broken through this slowly advancing semi-circle of men—one swift blow from his paw would have felled the strongest of them—but his main object was to get away from the noise. He hated and feared the noise made by humans.

He was not a man-eater and he would not attack a man unless he was very angry or very frightened; and as yet he was neither. He had eaten well, and he would have liked to rest—but there would be no rest for him until the men ceased their tremendous clatter and din.

Nandu and Chottu kept close to their elders, knowing it wouldn't be safe to go back on their own. Chottu felt sorry for the tiger.

'Do they have to kill the tiger?' he asked. 'If they drive him across the river he won't come back, will he?'

'Who knows?' said Nandu. 'He has found it's easy to kill our buffaloes, and when he's hungry he'll come again. We have to live too.'

Chottu was silent. He could see no way out for the tiger.

For an hour the villagers beat the jungle, shouting, drumming and trampling the undergrowth.

The tiger had no rest. Whenever he was able to put some distance between himself and the men, he would sink down in some shady spot to rest; but, within a few minutes, the trampling and drumming would come nearer, and with an angry snarl he would get up again and pad northwards, along the narrowing strip of jungle, towards the bridge across the river.

It was about noon when the tiger finally came into the open. The boys had a clear view of him as he moved slowly along, now in the open with the sun glinting on his glossy side, then in the shade or passing through the shorter grass. He was still out of range of Kundan Singh's gun, but there was no way in which he could retreat.

He disappeared among some bushes but soon reappeared to retrace his steps. The beaters had done their work well. The tiger was now only about a-hundred-and-fifty yards from the place where Kundan Singh waited.

The beat had closed in, the men were now bunched together. They were making a great noise, but nothing moved.

Chottu, watching from a distance, wondered: has he slipped through the beaters? And in his heart he hoped so.

Tins clashed, drums beat and some of the men poked into the reeds along the river bank with their spears or bamboo sticks. Perhaps one of these thrusts found its mark, because at last the tiger was roused, and with an angry, desperate snarl he charged out of the reeds, splashing his way through an inlet of mud and water.

Kundan Singh fired and missed.

The tiger rushed forward, making straight for the only way across the river—the suspension bridge that crossed it, providing a route into the hills beyond.

The suspension bridge swayed and trembled as the big tiger lurched across it. Kundan fired again, and this time the bullet grazed the tiger's shoulder.

The tiger bounded forward, lost his footing on the unfamiliar, slippery planks of the swaying bridge and went over the side, falling headlong into the swirling water of the river.

He rose to the surface once, but the current took him under and away, and before long he was lost to view.

5

At first the villagers were glad—they felt their buffaloes were safe. Then they began to feel that something had gone out of their lives, out of the life of the forest. The forest had been shrinking year by year, as more people had moved into the area; but as long as the tiger had been there and they had heard him roar at night, they had known there was still some distance between them and the ever-spreading towns and cities. Now that the tiger had gone, it was as though a protector had gone.

The boys lay flat on their stomachs on their little mud island, and watched the monsoon clouds gathering overhead.

'The king of the jungle is dead,' said Nandu. 'There are no more tigers.'

'There have to be tigers,' said Chottu. 'Can there be an India without tigers?'

The river had carried the tiger many miles away from his old home, from the forest he had always known, and brought him ashore on the opposite bank of the river, on a strip of warm yellow sand. Here he lay in the sun, quite still, breathing slowly.

Vultures gathered and waited at a distance, some of them perching on the branches of nearby trees. But the tiger was more drowned than hurt, and as the river water oozed out of his mouth, and the warm sun made new life throb through his body, he stirred and stretched, and his glazed eyes came into focus. Raising his head, he saw trees and tall grass.

Slowly he heaved himself off the ground and moved at a crouch to where the tall grass waved in the afternoon breeze. Would he be hunted again, and shot at? There was no smell of man. The tiger moved forward with greater confidence.

There was, however, another smell in the air, a smell that reached back to the time when he was young and fresh and full of vigour; a smell that he had almost forgotten but could never really forget—the smell of a tigress.

He lifted his head, and new life surged through his limbs. He gave a deep roar, 'A-oonh!' and moved purposefully through the tall grass. And the roar came back to him, calling him, urging him forward; a roar that meant there would be more tigers in the land!

That night, half asleep on his cot, Chottu heard the tigers roaring to each other across the river, and he recognised the roar of his own tiger. And from the vigour of its roar he knew that it was alive and safe; and he was glad.

'Let there be tigers forever,' he whispered into the darkness before he fell asleep.

A LITTLE WORLD OF MUD

I had never realised there was much to be found in the rainwater pond behind our house in North India except for large quantities of mud and sometimes a water-buffalo.

It was Grandfather who introduced me to the pond's diversity of life, so beautifully arranged that each individually gained some benefit from the well-being of the mass. To the inhabitants of the pond, the pond was the world; and to the inhabitants of the world, maintained Grandfather, the world was but a muddy pond.

When Grandfather first showed me the pond-world, he chose a dry place in the shade of an old peepul tree, where we sat for an hour, gazing steadily at the thin green scum on the water.

The buffaloes had not arrived for their afternoon dip, and the surface of the pond was still.

For the first ten minutes we saw nothing. Then a small black blob appeared in the middle of the pond; gradually it rose higher, until at last we could make out a frog's head, its great eyes staring hard at us. He did not know if we were friends or enemies and kept his body out of sight. A heron, his mortal enemy, might have been wading about in search of him.

When he had made sure we were not herons, he informed his friends and neighbours, and soon there were several big heads and eyes just above the surface of the water. Throats swelled, and a 'wurk, wurk, wurk' began.

In the shallow water near the tree we could see a dark shifting shadow. When touched with the end of a stick, the dark mass immediately became alive. Thousands of little black tadpoles wriggled into life, pushing and hustling each other.

'What do tadpoles eat?' I asked.

'They eat each other most of the time,' said Grandfather. 'It may seem an unpleasant custom, but when you think of the thousands of tadpoles that are hatched, you'll realise what a useful system it is. If all the young tadpoles in this pond became frogs, they'd take up every inch of ground between here and the house!'

'Their croaking would certainly drive Grandmother crazy,' I said.

All the same, I took home a number of frogs, placed them in a large glass jar, and left them on the window-sill of my bedroom.

At about four o'clock in the morning the entire household was awakened by a loud and fearful noise, and my grandparents, aunts and servants gathered on the verandah for safety. They were furious when they discovered that my frogs were the cause of the noise. Seeing the dawn breaking, the frogs had with one accord begun their morning songs.

Grandmother wanted to throw the frogs, bottle and all, out of the window; but Grandfather gave the bottle a good shaking and the frogs stayed quiet. Everyone went back to bed, but I was obliged to stay awake, to shake the bottle whenever the frogs showed signs of bursting into song. Long before breakfast,

I had let them loose in the garden.

I was soon visiting the pond on my own. Exploring its banks and shallows; and taking off my shoes, I would wade into the muddy water up to my knees, and pluck the water lilies floating on the surface.

One day, when I reached the pond. I found it occupied by buffaloes. Their owner, a boy a little older than me, was swimming about in the middle of the pond. He pulled himself up on the back of one of his buffaloes, stretched his slim brown body out on the animal's glistening back and started singing to himself.

When the boy saw me staring at him, he smiled, showing gleaming white teeth in his dark, sub-burnished face. He invited me into the water for a swim. I told him I couldn't swim, and he offered to teach me.

I hesitated, knowing that Grandmother held strict and rather old-fashioned views about my mixing with village children; but, deciding that Grandfather—who sometimes smoked a hookah on the sly—would get me out of any trouble that might arise, I took the bold step of accepting the boy's offer. And once taken, the step did not seem so very bold.

He dived off the back of his buffalo and swam across to me. And I, having removed my shirt and shorts, followed his instructions until I was floundering about among the water-lilies. His name was Ramu, and he promised to give me swimming lessons every afternoon; and so it was during the afternoons—especially summer afternoons when everyone was asleep—that we met.

Before long I was able to swim across the pond to sit with Ramu astride a contented buffalo, standing like an island in the middle of a muddy ocean. Sometimes we would try racing the buffaloes, Ramu and I sitting on different beasts.

But they were lazy creatures and would leave one comfortable spot only to look for another; or, if they were in no mood for games, would simply roll over on their backs, taking us with them into the mud and green slime of the pond. I would emerge from the pond in shades of green and khaki, slip into the house through the bathroom, and bathe under the tap before getting into my clothes. Ramu came from a family of low-caste farmers and had received no schooling. But he was well-versed in folklore and knew a great deal about birds and animals.

'Many birds are sacred,' he told me, as a bluejay swooped down from the peepul tree and carried off a grasshopper. Ramu said that both the bluejay and Lord Shiva were called 'Nilkanth'.

Shiva had a blue throat like the bird, because out of compassion for the human race, he had swallowed a deadly poison which was meant to destroy the world. Keeping the poison in his throat, he had not let it go further.

'Are squirrels sacred?' I asked.

'Lord Krishna loved them,' said Ramu. 'He would take them in his arms and stroke them with his long fingers. That is why they have four dark lines down their backs from head to tail. Krishna was very dark, and the lines are the marks of his fingers.'

Both Ramu and Grandfather felt that we should be more gentle with birds and animals, that we should not kill them indiscriminately.

'We must acknowledge their rights on the earth,' said Grandfather. 'Everywhere, birds and animals are finding it more difficult to live because we are destroying their forests.

They have to keep moving as the trees disappear.'

Ramu and I spent many long summer afternoons in the pond. We never saw each other again after I left my grandparents' house. He could not read or write, so we were unable to keep in touch. No one knew of our friendship.

Only the buffaloes and the frogs were our confidants. They had accepted us as part of their own world, their muddy but comfortable pond. And when I went away, both they and Ramu must have assumed that I would return again like the birds.

COPPERFIELD IN THE JUNGLE

Grandfather never hunted wild animals; he could not understand the pleasure some people obtained from killing the creatures of our forests. Birds and animals, he felt, had as much right to live as humans. There was some justification in killing for food—most animals did—but none at all in killing just for the fun of it.

At the age of twelve, I did not have the same high principles as Grandfather. Nevertheless, I disliked anything to do with shikar or hunting. I found it terribly boring.

Uncle Henry and some of his sporting friends once took me on a shikar expedition into the Terai forests of the Siwaliks. The prospect of a whole week in the jungle as camp follower to several adults with guns filled me with dismay. I knew that long, weary hours would be spent tramping behind these tall, professional-looking huntsmen. They could only speak in terms of bagging this tiger or that wild elephant, when all they ever got, if they were lucky, was a wild hare or a partridge. Tigers and excitement, it seemed, came only to Jim Corbett.

This particular expedition proved to be different from others. There were four men with guns, and at the end of the week, all that they had shot were two miserable, underweight wild fowls. But I managed, on our second day in the jungle, to be left behind at the rest house. And, in the course of a morning's exploration of the old bungalow, I discovered a shelf of books half-hidden in a corner of the back veranda.

Who had left them there? A literary forest officer? A memsahib who had been bored by her husband's camp-fire boasting? Or someone who had no interest in the 'manly' sport of slaughtering wild animals and had brought his library along to pass the time?

Or possibly the poor fellow had gone into the jungle one day, as a gesture towards his more bloodthirsty companions, and been trampled by an elephant, or gored by a wild boar, or (more likely) accidentally shot by one of the shikaris and his sorrowing friends had taken his remains away and left his books behind.

Anyway, there they were—a shelf of some thirty volumes, obviously untouched for many years. I wiped the thick dust off the covers and examined the titles. As my reading tastes had not yet formed, I was willing to try anything. The bookshelf was varied in its contents—and my own interests have since remained fairly universal.

On that fateful day in the forest rest house, I discovered P.G. Wodehouse and read his *Love Among the Chickens*, an early Ukridge story and still one of my favourites. By the time the perspiring hunters came home late in the evening, with their spent cartridges and lame excuses, I had made a start with M.R. James's *Ghost Stories of an Antiquary*, which had me hooked on ghost stories for the rest of my life. It kept me awake most of the night, until the oil in the kerosene lamp had finished.

Next morning, fresh and optimistic again, the shikaris set out for a different area, where they hoped to 'bag a tiger'. They had employed a party of villagers to beat the jungle, and all day I could hear their drums throbbing in the distance. This did not prevent me from finishing M.R. James or discovering a book called *A Naturalist on the Prowl* by Edward Hamilton Aitken.

My concentration was disturbed only once, when I looked up and saw a spotted deer crossing the open clearing in front of the bungalow. The deer disappeared among the sal trees, and I returned to my book.

Dusk had fallen when I heard the party returning from the hunt. The great men were talking loudly and seemed excited. Perhaps they had got their tiger. I put down my book and came out to meet them.

'Did you shoot the tiger?' I asked excitedly.

'No, my boy,' said Uncle Henry. 'I think we'll bag it tomorrow. But you should have been with us—we saw a spotted deer!'

◆

There were three days left and I knew I would never get through the entire bookshelf. So I chose *David Copperfield*—my first encounter with Dickens—and settled down on the veranda armchair to make the acquaintance of Mr Micawber and his family, Aunt Betsy Trotwood, Mr Dick, Peggotty, and a host of other larger-than-life people. I think it would be true to say that *David Copperfield* set me off on the road to literature; I identified with young David and wanted to grow up to be a writer like him.

But on my second day with the book, an event occurred which disturbed my reading for a little while.

I had noticed, on the previous day, that a number of stray dogs—belonging to watchmen, villagers and forest guards—

always hung about the house, waiting for scraps of food to be thrown away. It was ten o'clock in the morning, a time when wild animals seldom come into the open, when I heard a sudden yelp in the clearing. Looking up, I saw a large leopard making off into the jungle with one of the dogs held in its jaws. The leopard had either been driven towards the house by the beaters, or had watched the party leave the bungalow and decided to help itself to a meal.

There was no one else about at the time. Since the dog was obviously dead within seconds of being seized, and the leopard had disappeared, I saw no point in raising an alarm which would have interrupted my reading. So I returned to *David Copperfield*.

It was getting late when the shikaris returned. They were dirty, sweaty and as usual, disappointed. Next day we were to return to the city, and none of the hunters had anything to show for a week in the jungle. Swear words punctuated their conversation.

'No game left in these... jungles,' said the leading member of the party, famed for once having shot two man-eating tigers and a basking crocodile in rapid succession.

'It's this beastly weather,' said Uncle Henry. 'No rain for months.'

'I saw a leopard this morning,' I said modestly.

But no one took me seriously. 'Did you really?' said the leading hunter, glancing at the book beside me. 'Young Master Copperfield says he saw a leopard!'

'Too imaginative for his age,' said Uncle Henry. 'Comes from reading too much, I suppose.'

'If you were to get out of the house and into the jungle,' said the third member, 'you might really see a leopard! Don't know what young chaps are coming to these days.'

I went to bed early and left them to their tales of the 'good old days' when rhinos, cheetahs and possibly even the legendary phoenix were still available for slaughter.

Next day the camp broke up and we went our different ways. I was still only half-way through *David Copperfield*, but I saw no reason why it should be left behind to gather dust for another thirty years, and so I took it home with me. I have it still, a reminder of how I failed as a shikari but launched myself on a literary career.

THE FOUR FEATHERS

Our school dormitory was a very long room with about thirty beds, fifteen on either side of the room. This was good for pillow fights. Class V would take on Class VI (the two senior classes in our Prep school) and there would be plenty of space for leaping, struggling small boys, pillows flying, feathers flying, until there was a cry of 'Here comes Fishy!' or 'Here comes Olly!' and either Mr Fisher, the Headmaster, or Mr Oliver, the Senior Master, would come striding in, cane in hand, to put an end to the general mayhem. Pillow fights were allowed, up to a point; nobody got hurt. But parents sometimes complained if, at the end of the term, a boy came home with a pillow devoid of cotton-wool or feathers.

In that last year at Prep school in Shimla, there were four of us who were close friends—Bimal, whose home was in Bombay; Riaz, who came from Lahore; Bran, who hailed from Vellore; and your narrator, who lived wherever his father (then in the Air Force) was posted.

We called ourselves the 'Four Feathers', the feathers signifying that we were companions in adventure, comrades-in-arms and knights of the round table. Bimal adopted a peacock's feather as his emblem—he was always a bit showy. Riaz chose a falcon's feather—although we couldn't find one. Bran and I were at first offered crow's or murghi feathers, but we protested vigorously and threatened a walkout. Finally, I settled for a parrot's feather (taken from Mrs Fisher's pet parrot), and Bran found a woodpecker's, which suited him, as he was always knocking things about.

Bimal was all thin legs and arms, so light and frisky that at times he seemed to be walking on air. We called him 'Bambi', after the delicate little deer in the Disney film. Riaz, on the other hand, was a sturdy boy, good at games though not very studious; but always good-natured, always smiling.

Bran was a dark, good-looking boy from the South; he was just a little spoilt—hated being given out in a cricket match and would refuse to leave the crease!—but he was affectionate and a loyal friend. I was the 'scribe'—good at inventing stories in order to get out of scrapes—but hopeless at sums, my highest marks being 22 out of 100.

On Sunday afternoons, when there were no classes or organised games, we were allowed to roam about on the hillside below the school. The Four Feathers would laze about on the short summer grass, sharing the occasional food parcel from home, reading comics (sometimes a book) and making plans for the long winter holidays. My father, who collected everything from stamps to seashells to butterflies, had given me a butterfly net and urged me to try and catch a rare species which, he said, was found only near Chotta Shimla. He described it as a large purple butterfly with yellow and black borders on its wings. A Purple Emperor, I think it was called. As I wasn't very good at identifying butterflies, I would chase anything that happened to flit across the school grounds, usually ending up with Common Red Admirals, Clouded Yellows, or Cabbage Whites. But that

Purple Emperor—that rare specimen being sought by collectors the world over—proved elusive. I would have to seek my fortune in some other line of endeavour.

One day, scrambling about among the rocks, and thorny bushes below the school, I almost fell over a small bundle lying in the shade of a young spruce tree. On taking a closer look, I discovered that the bundle was really a baby, wrapped up in a tattered old blanket.

'Feathers, feathers!' I called, 'Come here and look. A baby's been left here!'

The feathers joined me and we all stared down at the infant, who was fast asleep.

'Who would leave a baby on the hillside?' asked Bimal of no one in particular.

'Someone who doesn't want it,' said Bran.

'And hoped some good people would come along and keep it,' said Riaz.

'A panther might have come along instead,' I said. 'Can't leave it here.'

'Well, we'll just have to adopt it,' said Bimal.

'We can't adopt a baby,' said Bran.

'Why not?'

'We have to be married.'

'We don't.'

'Not us, you dope. The grown-ups who adopt babies.'

'Well, we can't just leave it here for grows-ups to come along,' I said.

'We don't even know if it's a boy or a girl,' said Riaz.

'Makes no difference. A baby's a baby. Let's take it back to school.'

'And keep it in the dormitory?'

'Of course not. Who's going to feed it? Babies need milk. We'll hand it over to Mrs Fisher. She doesn't have a baby.'

'Maybe she doesn't want one. Look, it's beginning to cry. Let's hurry!'

Riaz picked up the wide-awake and crying baby and gave it to Bimal who gave it to Bran who gave it to me. The Four Feathers marched up the hill to school with a very noisy baby.

'Now it's done potty in the blanket,' I complained. 'And some of it's on my shirt.'

'Never mind,' said Bimal. 'It's for a good cause. You're a Boy Scout, remember? You're supposed to help people in distress.'

The headmaster and his wife were in their drawing room, enjoying their afternoon tea and cakes. We trudged in, and Bimal announced, 'We've got something for Mrs Fisher.'

Mrs Fisher took one look at the bundle in my arms and let out a shriek. 'What have you brought here, Bond?'

'A baby, ma'am. I think it's a girl. Do you want to adopt it?'

Mrs Fisher threw up her arms in consternation, and turned to her husband. 'What are we to do, Frank? These boys are impossible. They've picked up someone's child!'

'We'll have to inform the police,' said Mr Fisher, reaching for the telephone. 'We can't have lost babies in the school.'

Just then there was a commotion outside, and a wild-eyed woman, her clothes dishevelled, entered at the front door accompanied by several menfolk from one of the villages. She ran towards us, crying out, 'My baby, my baby! *Mera bachcha*! You've stolen my baby!'

'We found it on the hillside,' I stammered.

'That's right,' said Bran. 'Finder's keepers!'

'Quiet, Adams,' said Mr Fisher, holding up his hand for order and addressing the villagers in a friendly manner. 'These boys found the baby alone on the hillside and brought it here before...before...'

'Before the hyenas got it,' I put in.

'Quite right, Bond. And why did you leave your child alone?' he asked the woman.

'I put her down for five minutes so that I could climb the plum tree and collect the plums. When I came down, the baby had gone! But I could hear it crying up on the hill. I called the menfolk and we come looking for it.'

'Well, here's your baby,' I said, thrusting it into her arms. By then I was glad to be rid of it! 'Look after it properly in the future.'

'Kidnapper!' she screamed at me.

Mr Fisher succeeded in mollifying the villagers. 'These boys are good Scouts,' he told them. 'It's their business to help people.'

'Scout law number 3, sir,' I added. 'To be useful and helpful.'

And then the Headmaster turned the tables on the villagers. 'By the way, those plum trees belong to the school. So do the peaches and apricots. Now I know why they've been disappearing so fast!'

The villagers, a little chastened, went their way. Mr Fisher reached for his cane. From the way he fondled it, I knew he was itching to use it on our bottoms.

'No, Frank,' said Mrs Fisher, intervening on our behalf. 'It was really very sweet of them to look after that baby. And look at Bond—he's got baby-goo all over his clothes.'

'So he has. Go and take a bath, all of you. And what are you grinning about, Bond?'

'Scout law number 8, sir. A Scout smiles and whistles under all difficulties.'

And so ended the first adventure of the Four Feathers.

HAPPY BAZAAR

It was called 'Happy' Bus Stop because a local boy called 'Happy', happily drunk, had got into the driver's seat of the local bus and driven it over the edge of the cliff, onto the rocks some seventy feet below the road. Fortunately, the bus had been empty at the time, and only Happy and the vehicle had perished.

When I was a boy, the old road to Tehri had been little more than a footpath, and you walked from one village to the next. If you were in a hurry, you could take a ride on a mule—mules could navigate the narrowest of tracks—and reach your destination with a very sore bottom. It was wiser to walk.

Then, in mid-1962–63, after the Chinese incursions, there was a flurry of road-building in the hills, and the old footpaths and mule tracks were turned into motorways. A bus stop came up just outside the Landour boundary, and by 1970 there were buses to Chamba and beyond.

Where there is a bus stop you will find a tea shop, and if the tea shop prospers, it will be followed by another tea shop. Then there has to be a vegetable stand, because at the last moment bus passengers will remember to buy vegetables to take home. Sometimes they will fetch seasonal vegetables from their own villages to sell in the Landour market—cucumbers and beans during the monsoon rains, pumpkins and maize a little later. The vegetable stalls near the bus stop and in the town will have fruit and vegetables from all over the country—coconuts and pomegranates, pineapples and custard apples.

As the bus stop grew bigger, and the number of buses increased, the shops prospered. One tea shop specialised in pakoras, the other in samosas; the competition remained friendly.

Soon, a little chemist's shop was opened. After all, there was a hospital nearby, and sometimes the patients, or their relatives, required medicines that were not available from the hospital's small pharmacy. Sick and injured people from the surrounding villages would use the buses to come to the hospital. The town had one ambulance and this was usually engaged in bringing townspeople to the emergency ward. The ambulance had a loud, piercing siren, and people living along the main road would be woken up in the middle of the night, or in the early hours before daybreak, by the wail of the ambulance.

Early morning, the first bus left for Chamba. Late evening, the last bus arrived at 'Happy' Bus Stop. Gradually, the owners of the shops expanded their shacks into brick houses. They teetered over the side of the road, packed together like an upside-down Potala Palace.

By the 1990s there were at least ten shops (and residences) near the bus stop, and people began calling it a market. They had forgotten who 'Happy' was, but they called it the Happy Bazaar.

And presently a 'wine' shop opened, to relieve the thirst of bus drivers, passengers, shopkeepers, hospital patients and their relatives, and anyone who cared to stroll down Happy Bazaar. It wasn't strictly a wine shop, merely an outlet for country liquor.

If you wanted 'foreign liquor' (i.e. whisky or rum) you had to go to the 'English wine shop' in town, where you could get Indian-made foreign liquor.

The country liquor was strong stuff and sometimes fights broke out and accidents took place. An inebriated bus driver tried to take a shortcut to Chamba by avoiding the road altogether, with the result that both he and many of his passengers took a shortcut into their next incarnations.

Fortunately, there was a police outpost not too far away, and things did not get out of hand too often.

All went well for several years, and the population of Happy Bus Stop and Happy Bazaar grew and prospered. They did not pay much attention to the new road that was being built, a bypass that would provide an alternative route into the mountains. And one day, amidst much fanfare, a minister from the state's capital arrived and opened a new bus stop, a couple of miles from Happy Bazaar, and flagged off a brand new bus to Chamba and beyond.

The Happy Bus Stop continued to function—but not for long. The claims of the new bus stop were considered to be much stronger, and it had political backing, which made all the difference. One by one the buses and their crew moved on to the new site. There was a marked decline in the number of people who used the little marketplace. Fruit and vegetables piled up, and the owner of the vegetable stall was kept busy all day, dousing his wares with cold water in order to keep them fresh. One of the tea shops closed down, the owner renting premises at the new site. I remained loyal to the remaining tea shop, as I preferred pakoras to samosas, and besides, my home was close by.

I sat alone in the tea shop, keeping the owner company.

'Well, at least the mules are back,' said Melaram abruptly. He was always the optimist.

'This was always their road,' I said. 'They resent the cars and buses.'

The muleteers and local villagers helped to make up the loss of business, but it wasn't quite the same; they did not have much money to spend. Occasionally, Melaram would provide tea and pakoras to the relatives of patients who were in the hospital, and this kept him going. And the chemist's shop remained in business, and so did old Abdul the Bulbul (as he was called by the children) who made mattresses and razais for the hospital and local residents. But most of the time Happy Bazaar wore a forlorn look.

And then one day, as I was sitting in the tea shop, contemplating a dish of pakoras, a dapper-looking gentleman walked in and ordered a cup of tea. Melaram and I took notice. It was some time since a stranger had walked into the shop.

Over a glass of hot tea he seemed inclined to talk, although, when we asked him where he came from, he was rather vague and mentioned some town in Kyrgyzstan or Tajikistan, I'm not sure which, and told us his name was Dr Cosmo.

'You can call me Cosmos if you like,' he said with a brilliant smile. 'In reality I belong to the world. To the universe.'

'And what kind of doctor are you?' asked Melaram. 'Can you cure my rheumatism?'

'Of course,' said the stranger. 'But to tell the truth, I'm looking for a quiet place where I can rest from my labours. All this healing can be very taxing. But come closer. Tell me where it hurts. Is there a swelling?'

'In my wrist,' said Melaram. 'And in my elbow. It's worse at night. The pain prevents me from sleeping.'

'Give me your hand.'

Melaram presented his hand, and the stranger took it and held it for some time.

'Do you feel anything?' he asked.

'No.'

The stranger held it a little longer—long enough for me to finish my tea and pakoras.

'I feel a tingling,' said Melaram.

'Good. That's the energy from my body passing into you. It's called cosmic energy. It comes from the sun. It's absorbed by me, and I pass it on to you. You will sleep well tonight. There will be no pain. Now tell me where I can find a place to stay. I like the look of this place. It's restful, at peace with itself.'

'It's restful because most of the people have gone away,' said Melaram. 'This used to be a busy bus stop. But the bus stop was moved closer to the town, and most of our business has gone with it. There's no hotel here. But I have a spare room behind the shop. It used to be occupied by a tailor, but he's moved on too. It's a very simple room—too simple for you, perhaps.'

'The simpler the better,' said Dr Cosmo. 'A good bed, a clean bathroom and breakfast, perhaps?'

'His parathas are very good,' I chimed in.

'Then lead on, my friend. Show me your honeymoon suite.'

And the next day the good doctor—healer would be a better word—moved in, accompanied by just a few worldly possessions, or rather necessities, and absolutely no medicines or any indication that he was a conventional doctor.

But he liked being called 'doctor', and to one and all he would be known as 'Doctor Cosmos'.

◆

Melaram's rheumatic pains disappeared overnight, and he lost no time in telling his friends and neighbours of his tenant's healing powers. And it didn't take long for others with chronic disabilities to turn up at the tea shop seeking similar treatment.

Dr Cosmos obliged everyone. He laid his hands on you—on head or heart or back or foot or wherever the patient felt pain or weakness—and then gave the sufferer a few words of encouragement and sent him on his way. Soon people reported that they felt better; some even claimed to be cured. Cripples stood straight and walked with a spring in their step. Old women abandoned their wheelchairs and climbed steep hillsides on foot.

Word of the miraculous healings spread beyond the hill station, and soon the sick and weary from other parts of the land were making their way to Happy Bazaar in search of cures.

Dr Cosmos did not claim to be a faith healer or a dispenser of miracles. It had nothing to do with religion, he said. It was all cosmic energy. It passed through him and into the sufferer, and behold, the pains, the weariness, the ailments disappeared.

'You can try doing it yourself,' he said.

Well, I did try it, but without any success. I tried to cure an old woman's toothache by placing my hand on her cheek, and she brushed it away, saying I was a cheeky fellow and a fraud.

But no one accused Dr Cosmos of being a fraud. Not everyone got better or was returned to normal, but a good many did seem to benefit from his doses of cosmic energy, and he was in great demand. Before long he needed a couple of helpers and a large room, and these were provided by the bazaar people. They also persuaded him to accept a small fee from his patients to pay for his board and lodging.

A guest house came up to accommodate patients from other towns. It was built where the old bus stop had stood. Nearby

hotels and hostelries were reported to be full, even off season.
Cars rolled up with rich sufferers, ready to part with large sums
of money if they could be cured of chronic ailments, cancer
or diabetes or old injuries. And Dr Cosmos treated them too
but did not take any 'fees'.

Then some medical men persuaded him to come to Delhi to
demonstrate his 'powers', to lecture them on cosmic energy. He
made several trips to the capital. He was becoming famous. But
every time he returned from Delhi he looked a little thinner, a
little more frail, a bit like some of his patients. It was clear that
the capital's air or water or atmosphere did not agree with him.
He had become accustomed to the good, clean air of the hills.

'Up here, the cosmic energy flows without hindrance,' he
claimed.

'Then stay up here,' said Melaram. 'You can't cure all of
Delhi of their ailments. I don't go there myself. They should
move the capital elsewhere!'

'Someone tried that long ago,' I said. 'They moved to
Daulatabad. But it didn't work. I think they missed the dear
old Jamuna.'

So Dr Cosmos's trips to Delhi continued, and although his
fame grew, his own health deteriorated, so much so that I felt
tempted to say, 'Physician, heal thyself.'

When I heard that he had been admitted to one of the
capital's premier hospitals, with an 'unknown' and unspecified
complaint, I went down to see him, accompanied by Melaram.

Lying there in his hospital bed, he looked desiccated, devoid
of life's juices. This was not the Dr Cosmos we knew. He was
barely recognisable. His cheeks were sunken, his teeth missing,
his hair falling out. But he recognised us, and raised his hand
in a feeble greeting.

'What happened to you?' I asked.

He shook his head, whispered: 'I took on too much. Now I have all the diseases in the world. It's a wonderful thing, in a way. Absorbing their fits and fevers, giving them energy in return.'

'Cosmic energy,' I said. 'You should have kept some for yourself.'

He nodded. 'I will recover. I will regain my strength as soon as I am back in the mountains.'

But he did not return to the mountains. Melaram and I had to return without him. He was too far gone. And a week later we heard that he had joined the cosmos. Some of his relatives turned up and buried him in a corner of a Delhi cemetery; there is no tombstone to mark the place, no record of his fleeting presence on planet earth. No cause of death had been given; but the medical report did mention that traces of strontium had been found in his blood. How did this obscure metallic element get into his system? Had it something to do with the cosmic energy he radiated? We shall never know. There will always be mysteries.

◆

It was thought that the passing of Dr Cosmos would affect the popularity of Happy Bazaar as a destination for tourists. But this did not happen. Curious visitors continued to come our way, many of them eager to see the humble room in which the healer had first seen his patients and sent them happily on their way, bursting with cosmic energy. Some felt that by touching his desk or chair or bed they would obtain relief from their various ailments. And perhaps they did. For thought is a wonderful thing, and mind can prevail over matter.

Happy Bazaar continued to prosper, and so did Melaram, for he owned the premises, and although he did not charge an entry fee, visitors would spend some time in his tea shop, sampling his tea and pakoras. No one made better pakoras.

I was present when a local guide brought a group of tourists into the shop, and expounded on the history of Happy Bazaar, telling them how it had gained its reputation for happiness because of the miracles performed by the now legendary doctor.

I tried to interrupt and tell them that the bazaar had in fact got its name from the delinquent youth 'Happy' who had driven a bus over a nearby cliff. But no one was listening to me.